Straight Outta DC Productions Presents....

Still In Love with The Queen of DC

Prologue

I had so much shit going through my head I needed answers to. Had anybody seen me this morning? Who had burned down our shit? And Lastly, why was Keeli out here lying about her name and more importantly, what the fuck was her connection to this nigga Detective Donald Bell. I was really hoping I aint just kill this nigga over no pussy cause that would've been crazy.

Finally, the story I had been waiting to see hit the news. The police chief and the mayor were gathered with what looked like every fucking officer to ever be sworn in as a part of MPD were gathered outside of Washington Hospital Center for a press conference on what happened this morning. This was one time the police had my undivided attention...

"This morning, at approximately 7:45am, a decorated detective from our very own 5th District was shot multiple times during a routine traffic stop. Our detective, whose name is not being released at this time sustained multiple life threatening injuries. He is currently in surgery where

he is fighting for his life. At this time, we are asking the public, if you were in the area of the 1600 Block of Lyman place this morning and happened to see anything at all, we are asking that you come forward immediately. At the present time we do not have any information on the suspect. We are also unsure if this was firefight or an ambush. Until the public comes forward or our detective is out of surgery and stable, we have no further information to give."

I turned the TV off because I knew one of two things was happening and neither was good. Either the Chief of Police was standing on TV lying and Detective Bell was dead as I suspected, because I gave that nigga the entire clip… or he really had somehow miraculously not died yet and was really in surgery fighting for his life. Either way, I wasn't trying to be around when they either stop bullshitting and announced his death or he really did come out of surgery alive and well. I knew exactly what I had to do then. Wasn't no two ways about that shit.

I slept in spells that night. Sporadically watching the news and wrestling with my own thoughts. By the next morning, the story was that Bell was still in life threatening condition. Before shit got worse I decided I needed to get the fuck out. I rode with Lonnie the next day as he took the rental car, covered on his flatbed from DC down to McDuff, Virginia where his peoples owned a junk yard. I needed to see this car destroyed because although Lonnie was my folks, I wasn't leaving shit to chance. So I need to see this whole car disappear and it did in his peoples crusher machine.

We got back to DC late that night and the news was still reporting the same shit as far as his condition. They upped the anti and said they had a description of the suspect vehicle but oddly, they hadn't released it. I knew then it was bullshit and with that I borrowed one of Lonnie's car and went back up to Jersey. I had my mother to report that rental car stolen before they really did release a description it… and I needed to see my family before I got low.

Of course I told Roc and Mikey what was really going down, but my moms and daughter I just told them I had to get low. My mother knew shit like this came with the territory, so she promised me she had my daughter. I hated leaving TiTi and I was hoping I didn't have to stay gone long, but I would rather get low and be able to come back to her one day than stay put and end up spending the rest of my life in a fucking box… above or below ground. So after my mother reported the rental car stolen, I drove back to DC and went straight to the private airport in Leesburg with nothing but the clothes on my back and bid farewell to the place I had learned to call home and the woman who would forever be etched in my brain…..

Until I could see them again, which I was praying was sooner rather than later.

Still

In

Love

With

The

Queen

Of

D.C.

Chapter One

"Leaving DC was the hardest thing I had to do in a long time, but it was either that or end up in jail for murdering or attempting to murder a detective. Either way, I wasn't trying to be around when the shit hit the fan. I got the airport and had to wait while they arranged the flight crew. I was nervous as fuck pacing back and forth, waiting to see a shit storm of police cars coming down the runway at full speed to lock my dumb ass up. I looked for that shit constantly until I was finally up in the air on my way back home. Once we hit cruising altitude, I laid back and relaxed a bit, but not much though, because I already knew Ian was gonna have a whole fucking fit once he got wind to the shit that was going on.

When I stepped off the plane, there was a SUV waiting to take me to the King. I kept expecting him to call while we were in the air considering the pilot had to call ahead to get clearance for us to land, and once that call was *put in, they would notify my pops immediately. I wasn't scheduled to come home so he had to know something was wrong… but he never called. And that alone made each second tick by slower and my heart race faster.*

The over an hour-long ride to the main house on my dad's compound felt like it only took 20 minutes top. I said a quick prayer that Ian and I didn't have to lock asses today because the bottom line was, I did what I needed to do to stay the fuck alive. And furthermore, if his niece wasn't a dumb fucking slut, I would've never been on this nigga radar to begin with. So, if he really wanted to toss his weight around with anybody it needed to be that bitch.

I walked in the house and he was coming down the stairs followed by two bitches straight out the motherland. They both were tall, dark and stacked. That was one thing my father and I definitely had in common. We had a thing for dark skin women. It was something about them that did it for us. I was standing there mesmerized by all that chocolate draping over my father, and for the first time since my plane took off from the airport in Leesburg, I thought about the woman who was at the helm of why the fuck I was here. Fucking Keeli N. Byrd.

I missed her like shit, and it seemed like even being on the other side of the world wasn't going to change that, but now I was too hot to do anything but be where I was. It was no way I wasn't gonna get to the bottom of why the fuck Bell had somebody following her, or why the fuck she was out here lying about her name. But right now, I was here and had to let the heat die down. It's crazy that while I was thinking about the heat dying down all the way back in DC, I could see the heat rising in my father's face as his eyes burned a hole through me as he descended the winding staircase."

"When my telephone rung asking for clearance, I never thought it would be your plane number they were reading back to me." Pops said to me while shaking his head, making me feel like shit. "Come, let's talk." He tossed over his shoulder at me as he started down the hall leaving the bitches at the foot of the stairs. I reluctantly started to follow my dad down the hall to his office. The tension was so thick you could cut that shit with a knife. We walked through the huge double doors and entered Pops office. He sat behind his desk and I sat on the other side facing him. I wanted to jump right into the shit that had gone down, but I knew how my father operated. Although I was his first-born son, I had fucked up royally, so I sat back in the chair trying not to let the deadly gaze and deafening silence my father gave me push me over the edge. For a full 180 seconds, Ian said nothing. He just stared at me, making an already tensed situation feel a hundred times worse.

"Speak… and do not bullshit me Juan." Pops finally spoke in a tone that was commanding.

"I wont." I responded feeing, feeling chastised but matching his tone. "Simply put, I shot a cop."

"Ay Yi Yi." He shook his head in disbelief.

"Pops, I had no choice. It was either him or me and I did what I had to do to stay alive."

"Is he dead son?"

"I honestly don't know. I got low before all the details came out. Last I heard on the news he was in surgery and…"

"I don't understand Juan. How did you end up in this situation son? You could not have been dirty because you were on vacation and you know the rules."

"Of course, I know the rules. I wasn't in Jersey. I was in DC. I left because things were just...." Juan gets quiet.

"JUST WHAT!" Pops yelled and banged his fist on the desk hard enough to show me he wasn't fucking around while knocking down a few family photos he kept surrounding his workspace. "Let me tell you something, you show up here, telling me you shot a fucking cop, you don't even know if he's fucking dead or alive and you actually think you are not gonna give me every fucking detail of what brought this bullshit on?"

"I didn't say that."

"Then fucking start talking and don't leave out a Goddamn detail."

"I took a deep breath to check my own anger that was boiling because father or not, Ian was getting out of pocket with the way he was coming at me about this shit. Like I said I was in a fucking kill or be killed situation and I did what the fuck I had to do. I was sitting there looking at my father wondering if he would have rather, I had fucking died out there in that alley. Okay deep in my heart I knew I was reaching with that but I'm like damn, this dude really was about to try and take

my whole fucking head off Pops. Lighten the fuck up already. But I gave him the rundown, and while he was demanding that I give him "every fucking detail" and in most situations I would have... but this one, I couldn't.

I found myself omitting any and everything that had to do with Keeli. I didn't want her name mixed up in this shit at all because I knew my father and even though he was giving me grief right now, it was very possible a war was on the horizon. Yeah, she had been a lying whore during our relationship, but I still loved her.

After I told my father what was what... what I wanted him to know anyway, he dismissed me while he got on the ball. That was only after he gave me shit about not legit having police in pocket in DC. He spent about 30 minutes harping on how that was the problem with our generation we ran around screaming fuck the police when in all actuality, we NEEDED legit cops on our payroll. I always felt like we were careful enough that we didn't need no fucking bitch ass police with their hands in our pockets. You see what that shit got me dealing with Bell. It never ended good if you asked me. I felt like having my sisters who were attorneys standing by my side was enough. You better believe Tia checked databases etcetera, frequently for our names to see if we had made the list. I always felt like that was enough. Pops didn't.

Now, because of my lack of police presences, Ian had to go to the states. He was PISSED about that, but it was what it was.

My father left for DC three days after I got to Bogota, and for three weeks I waited on edge for his return. Yeah I enjoyed all the perks that came with being at his compound, the bitches, the staff, the chance to get my head clear and all that... but I still waited on edge to hear what the word was back in DC. Did this bitch ass nigga die? Was there a needle waiting with my name on it? What the fuck was really going on?

When my dad got back, I was on his heels wanting to know what the fuck was going on. But in true Ian Moreno fashion, he made me wait until he was ready to talk about shit. His old ass was really pissing me off and I swear if it wasn't for the fact that I knew that Colombia was not in the business of honoring extradition request from the United States, I probably wouldn't even have come here immediately. I just wanted to know what was what so I could decide how to play this and hopefully go back sooner rather than later.

Finally, after being home for a week and giving me absolutely nothing... like not even speaking to me, Ian summoned me to his office to clue me in on the mess that kicked up back in DC. I walked into his office and sat across from him just as I did on the day I arrived. And just as he did on that day, he made me sit in silence, stress and agony waiting for him to speak. Finally, after feeling like I had counted every gray in his beard one by one, he decided I was worthy of knowing my fucking fate.

"So, I have finally gotten the call I have been waiting for. And your copper, he's still alive. Apparently, he is making quite the miraculous discovery. I hear there was a news conference and all with him and his bandages sitting front and center."

"Damn." I banged the desk in frustration. "I gave him the whole fucking clip, how the fuck did he not die Pops?" I asked sincerely because I really didn't understand this shit.

"I don't know son. I guess it was just not his time. Which sucks for you."

"Yeah I know. So how will we play this Pops? Because his ass gotta GO. Immediately. I can't have this fake RoboCop ass nigga putting my name in a file."

"Relax son, a couple of things. Him putting your name in a file is something we don't have to worry about. The news is reporting that it was a traffic stop gone wrong. If he gives them a name, he then has to explain how he knows it. And from what my sources are telling me, he is gonna want this to go away quickly and quietly.

"Why is that?" I questioned because none of it was adding up for me. "Because I really can't see a supposedly decorated detective getting shot going away quickly and quietly."

"The description of the suspect he gave doesn't match you at all. He's saying a heavy-set dark skin man in a blue SUV shot him. And also, there is supposed to be a bunch of holes in his story. Like why he was shot 9 times, but only one bullet was found on the ground, at the other end of the alley, closer to his car. There is the matter of car window glass with traces of blood… his blood in that same area, but not near where he was found at. So, they are definitely looking further into the shit… but right now, the focus is more on why the fuck he's lying."

. "Yeah cause it aint like his ass can say 'Well I was sitting in the front seat with the nigga who shot me'." I didn't want to be smiling because I didn't want Pops to spaz, but one spread across my face so fast. I was legit happy they were taking the time to focus more on him and his bullshit story than who actually pulled the trigger

"Exactly. So, relax a bit. I'm sure your friend will be as quiet as a church mouse on this shit."

"You right. So, I can dip now?"

"Dip?" Pops asked in a tone and look that let me know that he was legit confused on what I was saying to him.

"Leave pops." I chuckled at his ignorance to slang. "Since this shit is quiet as kept, I can go home now. I miss my baby girl like crazy."

"She misses you too son. She's getting so big too."

"I can't believe Ma let you see her."

"Please don't ruin my mood by bringing up that vile woman." When Pops got up and went to the bar in his office and started to mae drinks, I could feel shit was not about to go in my favor. "But no son. You will not be going back to DC right now. Since you are already here, you can handle the orders and then I'm gonna send you out West for a while. At least a year or two."

"Are you fucking serious Pops?" I snapped instantly. "So I hit this nigga to stay alive and you still punishing me?"

"You call it punishment and I call it discipline." He responded to my emotional yelling with a cool and even tone which let me know he was being spiteful as fuck with this move. "You have too much going on back in DC, so I need you far away from there until everything is calm again. Mikey will take care of things on the East Coast. You will head to Seattle and handle the West.

"Pops. Come on man, you are killing me." I pleaded, damn near on the brink of tears at the thought of this shit.

"You will thank me eventually son. Trust me." I didn't even respond to that bullshit. I was trying not to go completely off the deep end because he knew this shit wasn't right. DC was my home. I had a daughter there to which I was her only fucking parent. He was foul as shit for this move. But it was his house, and his chess board so that meant I had no choice but to play b his rules. I finally blew out air in defeat which I guess signaled to him that I had accepted that this was now my fate and wasn't shit I could do about it. "Now that we got that under control, meet me in an hour for some golf." He said to me with a smug ass smile dancing around in his eyes.

"Yeah alright." I got up and walked out to keep from losing my shit completely.

"I left my dad office and went back to my room to process this bullshit before I went to meet my him for golf. I didn't give a fuck about playing no golf right now at all. Like he was real live sending me to the place I hated. Y'all already know how I felt about Seattle, and now to have to live there for years. Just the thought alone was blowing the shit out of me.

I got back to my room and sat down on the bed and closed my eyes, just trying to meditate the stress and anger off my brain. When I closed my eyes, out of nowhere, the memory of the day Keeli and I took the kids out to dinner and shit popped in my head. The smiles on all four of our faces was clear as day, just as was the laughs we shared. That day I knew what it felt like to have a family of my own and as crazy as it sounds, I still wanted it. And I wanted it with her. Yeah, I know her ass was the reason I was sitting in the predicament I was in now, but it didn't change how I felt about her. I decided then that I was okay with heading out West. At least then I would be back in the States. I could get my daughter and bring her out there for summer breaks and shit. I would also have a chance to get shit right with Keeli. And once I got her to move out there with me, I could bring TiTi home for good too. Yeah a nigga was planning for the long haul. So with that in my head I went on and got ready for Golf with my pops.

I stayed at the compound for another month. I got the next shipment together because I was out this bitch with nothing but time on my hands, so I handled it. That way when Mikey and Roc came over, we all had time to just chill and catch up. I missed them niggas bout as much as I missed Infinity and Keeli. They stayed over for two weeks just because and we played catch up about the shit that was going on back home. Apparently, Niema was pregnant and going crazy because nobody would tell her where the fuck I was. That pissed me off because my situation was complicated enough without this bitch who I also felt held blame in the way shit went down screaming she was pregnant all of a sudden.

Roc and Niyah had been staying together at a spot he had in the city since the house burnt down. Living with her sister gave him an insider advantage to watch for treachery because I personally was finding this pregnancy to be mighty convenient to say the least. So Roc was now my eyes and ears on her situation. I was just praying his judgement aint get clouded since he now had Niyah scrambling his eggs in the morning and sucking his dick at night.

Mikey and Shane were also living together now since the house burnt down. In a way I guess it worked out for everybody but me cause while these niggas got to take steps forward in their respective relationships, my ass was on the other side of the world getting ready to head into isolation which was some bullshit. The fire at the house had been ruled electrical and the case was closed. We decided to use the insurance payout to rebuild and then sell it because none of us were willing to go back there. Whoever started that fire had ruined that spot for all of us.

Once we were all caught up on the personal side of things, we moved on the business side of shit. Since I couldn't come back to DC right now, they were gonna have to handle the whole East Coast without me. I decided in order to be safe rather than sorry, we were done flying the shit into North Carolina. We would now use an airport in Sussex County Delaware. It was closer than North Carolina so that meant the shit was on the road less time which was safer for us. The guys also needed to find a new distribution spot. The same way Bell had motherfuckas following either me or Keeli so close and so undetected they were able to get an intimate photo that put our relationship in prospective for whoever wanted to know, he could've easily had a nigga follow me to the distribution center. Last thing I needed was for my family to get jammed up, so it was time to switch shit up. I also instructed them to sell off whatever was stored at the current distribution center for 5,000 a brick. That was dirt cheap but I didn't care. I just wanted the shit gone. The new plan was to never have no product on hand just in case Bell buffed up and shit really hit the fan. So, it was coke on hand for 24 hours tops moving forward.

Before we parted ways and they went home and I headed to Seattle, I asked Mikey to do me a favor and look in on Keeli from time to time. Don't let her know he was looking in but to do so. I opted not to tell them how her name was mixed up in this shit with Detective Bell also because until I knew what the fuck was going on with that, I didn't need nobody else speculating on their connection or painting me with the brush of a fool. With that, we all parted ways. They went back to DC and I went to Seattle. My fucking suitcase barely stopped rocking before shit was all fucked up again.

Like the dummy I was proving myself to be, I sent for Niema. She was pregnant and I was lonely, so I figured why not. She left everything behind and moved out West with me. I thought about bringing my daughter also because I missed her little ass like crazy, but something in my heart of hearts wouldn't let me uproot her whole life and make her start over just because I had fucked up TREMENDOUSLY. So, it was Niema and I making a go of it out Seattle.

I talked to Mikey often about Keeli and he hadn't been able to catch up with her. I was feeling some kinda way about that, but I figured her and her dude, the nigga Simm were making a go of it just like Niema and I. So, I told him to stop looking for her. The shit just wasn't in the cards for us. If it was, she would've been here with me starting a family and not Niema's ass.

Unlike when I watched Maranda's belly swell with life, I felt no connection, no excitement about Niema's pregnancy. So much so I was regretting bringing her out here with me as well as not being around when she first discovered she was pregnant. It was no way I would've let her keep the baby because I really didn't want to keep her ass. She kept pushing the marriage issue, like trying hard to get me to say 'Okay lets do this since we were having a baby.'... but I couldn't. I managed to find me a few bitches out in Seattle to occupy my time and dick because it was like the further along Niema got in her pregnancy, the less I wanted her or wanted to be around her.

Shit back in DC had been quiet. It was like the shooting with Detective Bell just faded from the spotlight. There were no more news clippings, no more fake leads, no more anything surrounding the shooting of that decorated Detective.

In December, my family went to Germany for Christmas. It may seem like a strange vacation spot to some, but Ian had family there. His great grandparents were German. My family history was a motherfucka, but that's another story for another time. I didn't take Niema with me because all this time and the chick still didn't have a passport. I went with my family and she went back to DC to visit her family for the holiday. I was hoping that when I got back to Seattle, she'd called me and say she couldn't bare to be away from her family any longer. I mean she was getting ready to give birth to her first child, which was due March 8th… Keeli's birthday. I felt like she should want to be with her peoples.

I had no such luck.

I got home on a Sunday at 3:30pm and by 5pm her flight was landing bringing her ass back from DC. She came home with so much petty gossip from her bum ass sisters about what was going on in DC, and I cared about none of it. Then she hit me with some news that grabbed my attention, just as I am sure she knew it would."

"Oh, I know what I almost forgot to tell you." Niema started with a smirk on her face as she unpacked her dirty laundry. "You know somebody killed that bitch we broke up over."

"Who?" I asked as my heart fell in my stomach with my mind immediately going to Keeli.

"How the fuck am I supposed to know who killed the bitch Juan and more importantly why the fuck do you care?"

"Bitch…" I hopped up from the spot I had been sitting in on the bed, grabbed Niema by her neck and slammed her ass into the wall before she even realized what was happening. "I asked you a fucking question. WHAT BITCH NIEMA?" I screamed in her face. I had lost complete control just at the thought of something happening to Keeli. I couldn't take that shit and needed her to speak with clarity ASAP. It wasn;t even registering to me how tight my grip on her throat was as she clawed at my hand, trying to pry it off her neck. It wasn't until I saw the light in her eyes starting to fade that I realized I was gonna kill her. A part of me said fuck it and wanted to continue with the mission I had been assigned obviously. If I killed her ass, I wouldn't have to pretend to be in this relationship a second longer or be a father to a child she fucking KNEW I didn't want. Yeah, killing this bitch felt like the move. But then the reality of not ever getting whatever information she had that could have possibly concerned Keeli set in and I reluctantly released her ass.

She fell to the floor all dramatic like, and that shit did nothing but piss me off more. I wanted to just stomp this bitch head in and then drive her ass out to Pugent Sound and make her fucking disappear. She was down on the floor, doubled over while hacking up shit, gagging and crying all at the same time. I was ready to snatch this bitch bald and just beat the fuck out of her, but then she finally summoned the strength to respond. "The college bitch Juan! The nasty little bitch that left her discharged filled panties under your bed after you cheated on me and fucked that nasty bitch!" Her dumb ass screamed all loud as she jumped her big ass up off the floor pointng herNiema shouts at him pointing her fucking finger in my face.

I didn't even realize I let out a sigh of relief until I heard it echo in my ears. I was just glad it wasn't Keeli she was reporting bout and I couldn't hide that. I loved that woman. I knew from the look on Niema's face that in a sense I had showed my hand, and she hopped on that shit immediately. "Oh okay, I get it now. You thought somebody killed that other bitch we broke up behind. The one that fucked up your car and burned down the house."

"First it was an electrical fire that burned down the house and she didn't break us up, you and your fuck ass bullshit did!" I defended Keeli and her bullshit without a second thought. I decided then I needed to get the fuck away from Niema before I really killed her that night. I walked out the bedroom and started down the hall and her big ass was right behind me.

"Bullshit nigga! We were happy and planning a fucking wedding until that bitch showed up that night."

"If you thought I was happy Niema you clearly don't know me at all. Again, she didn't break us up, you did by running off at the mouth like you doing now."

"What the fuck is your deal with this bitch? You stay fucking defending her! This bitch tore up your whole fucking car and you broke up with ME instead of killing that bitch dead on the spot! I don't understand it. Do you love her Juan? Do you fucking want her here with you instead of me? Nigga let me know.

"Niema chill, you gonna get yourself all worked up and end up in the hospital or something. I tried to difuse the situation as I poured my bottle of water into a glass.

"No fuck that! I want to know! Would you rather that bitch be here instead of me?" She was screaming and crying and breathing all hard. I was so exhausted with all this shit and seriously regretted the day I let her the fuck in my life.

"Niema, please don't ask questions you don't really want the answer to." I answered her question without even answering her question because I knew she couldn't handle hearing how I truly felt about Keeli. Just the thought of it had this bitch ready to walk a mile into the Pacific Ocean.

"I walked away from Niema leaving her standing there with a hurt heart. I went and put on my shoes and grabbed my keys and just left. I needed to clear my head and I needed confirmation on what Niema had just told me. If Penny had really been found dead, I needed details. Because it was very well possible that while I didn't end her life, hadn't seen the bitch since I had her ass beat on her job... it could very well be set to look like I did as the Good Detective I tried to kill promised me it would.

I drove around for a little bit and then called Mikey and sure enough, Penny had been found dead. The body "washed up" on the Potomac River the day after Christmas. And apparently, Detective Bell had caught her case and was out here giving news conference. This nigga was sick. Mikey said this nigga was quoted in the paper saying how the person who took the life of this innocent college student would be brought to Justice at all cost. They were having a candlelight vigil up on the campus of Howard that night and Mikey said he was going. I wasn't sure why but trying to figure my own shit out prevented me from asking him. Maybe if I had, I would've been able to head this shit off before it went left, and my brother took matters in his own hands.

That night when I got back home, I slept in the guest room. It was late and Niema was already asleep and besides, I really didn't want to be near her. So I camped out in the guest room. I was awakened around 4am from a ringing phone. When I saw it was Tia's number I knew something was wrong."

"Hey sis, what's wrong?" I asked, bracing myself for whatever news was on the other end of her hello.

"Listen, I need you to get dressed and get to the airport NOW. Shit officially hit the fan and your brother caught one last night. Its tied to that other thing. So, go NOW!

"Fuck! Alright I'm getting up now. How is he?"

"I don't know yet. We will talk soon. Call me when you get to a safe place."

"I will Sis. Love you."

"Love you too little brother."

"I hung up the phone and had to take a moment to get my head right. I walked in the bedroom and saw Niema laying there sleeping peacefully. I didn't want to wake her for a multitude of reasons. The main one being I wasn't taking her with me. I couldn't. I was going back to my Father's compound and she could never step foot there. But I knew she wouldn't understand. I wrote her a note telling her something happened, and I would call her soon and that I loved her and not to worry... everything would be alright. That's what I wrote but that wasn't how I felt.

I didn't even know that fuck was going on. All I knew is my brother had caught a body and somehow, some way, it was connected to Detective Bell. So with that, I jumped in my car and drove out to the private airport. It took 5 hours before I could get off the ground, but once again I was headed back to face my father about some bullshit.

When I got to the compound, I had already mentally prepared for Ian old ass to be all in his chest about the shit that was going down, and he didn't disappoint your boy for sure. As soon as I walked through the door, he was going ape shit about how Mikey and I were trying to kill him. He said that's the only reason he could come up with us fucking up so severely these last few. I was about 20 seconds from bucking back because Ian had me fucked up this go round. I was way out West where he sent me and still didn't know what the fuck had gone on with Mikey ass. All I knew is my sister had told me to get low and that's what the fuck I did.

It took a few hours, but I finally got the run down on why I was being forced to be here watching Ian pace a path in the floor, all while taking shot after shot and calling us everything but children of God. On my soul if this nigga hadn't given me life, I would've shot his ass repeatedly, but he was Pops. So as irritated as I was, I remained quiet and just waited to hear what was up with my brother.

Finally, we got the story from Roc that Detective Bell bitch ass was leading a whole candlelight vigil for Penny. Out here claiming he would stop at nothing to bring justice to this young woman and her family. This nigga was different kind of sick I swear. Like nigga just arrest your motherfucking self because YOU DID THIS. Anyway, Mikey and some of his dudes had went to the vigil because he was keeping his eyes on this situation for me, and he just lost it. I guess knowing this bitch ass nigga standing behind the microphone was the cause of all the fuck shit happening in our lives was too much for little bro and his reckless ass started firing right then and there.

They arrested his ass ON SIGHT of course. The story was being painted that it was some neighborhood beef shit that spilled over into the vigil for this college student. I was thanking God they hadn't realized they had the shit so wrong and he was gunning for the lead detective on this case. Nobody actually got hit which was another blessing, so at that point he was just being charged with the gun and discharging a firearm. But with everything that was happening, my sister thought it was best that I got low just in case somebody was smart enough to make the connection that my cousin had a whole charge for beating the same bitch that turned up dead...

That I was fucking...

Who vigil my little brother had just shot up...

And lets not forget that the bitch burnt me…

And the bitch ass lead detective on her case was a nigga I filled with lead.

Yep it was best that my ass was not on U.S soil if anybody ever solved this mystery.

I stayed with my dad for a month and during that time, we started setting up shit for what was going to be my new normal. With Mikey in jail, Ian decided I was safer out of the U.S altogether. But being as though I still had a business that had to be ran, we agreed that I would set up in Panama. I left damn near immediately for my move to Panama. Missing a beat in getting that money wasn't an option so I got right on shit. I didn't talk to Niema again until I got to Panama and she was so hurt that I just left her. I felt like shit listening to her go off about how she just woke up and I was gone and how her blood pressure had been up, and her doctor was talking about inducing her early because she couldn't pull herself together and was becoming a risk to the baby. Listening to her tell me that shit just made me fucking mad all over again. At first I was feeling bad about the way I up and left her but this weak ass shit she was talking about was pissing me off. She sat on the phone and begged me to come back home and I told her I couldn't. She started trying to guilt trip me about me missing the birth of our baby and while I felt bad about shit, I wasn't about to get myself caught up by coming back. She told me then if I didn't come back she was gonna go back to DC with her family because she didn't want to be alone. I understood so I gave her my blessing to do so, but I guess that wasn't what she wanted to hear because she went completely off. I had enough shit on my plate where I wasn't checking for this bitch and her drama so I just hung up and went back to being a missing part of her lift as I had been for almost two months now.

My birthday rolled around and me and my niggas met up in Brazil to celebrate. With all that had been going on, I needed a vacation. Brazil was beautiful as always and I partied like a motherfucka, but none of that erased the fact that I knew the next day was the woman of my dreams birthday and I couldn't even reach out to her at this point. I aint gonna bullshit you, I had tried *but it was like her little black ass had just vanished from the face of the earth. Roc couldn't find her and none of her numbers worked anymore. Thinking about her made the day after my birthday hard to deal with. I kinda just stayed in my room with my dick buried deep in two Brazilian bitches who names I didn't even know. I know it was reckless, but it was all that kept me from thinking about Keeli and wherever she might have been at this point in life. I was really sick behind this bitch.*

On the morning of the 9th of March 1996 I woke up and was looking forward to the shit we had planned to do. I showered and got dressed and left my room and headed downstairs to get breakfast at the hotel restaurant. A few of my niggas was already down there so I was playing catch up on what they had got into the day before. Nobody knew why I opted out of the festivities, I just let them think I was too tied up with the bitches I took back to the room with me. Little did they know them bitches were nothing more than a distraction to keep my mind off the one that got away. Hell nah I couldn't let them niggas know Keeli stanking ass had me love sick out this bitch. I ordered my breakfast while I listened to these niggas tell me about the wilding that took place while I was hold up in room 612 all day yesterday. As soon as the waitress brought my food and I cast a blessing over the omlette that I was about to crush, Roc came bopping into the restaurant and I could tell by the look on his face that something was wrong.

"You good my nigga?" I asked Roc as he come up to the table and stood next to me.

"Nah, not really. I just got off the line with Niyah."

"She alright?" I didn't really care about her ass, but I knew she mattered to him so I faked concern.

"Yeah, she is, but Niema not. She went in for a checkup yesterday and the baby didn't have a heartbeat Slim.

"For real?" Was the only response my mind could form.

"Yeah. They induced her labor but…" He hesitated and looked off sadly which both scared me and aggravated me in the same breath.

"But what nigga!" I screamed on him.

"Motherfucka you need to go call that girl. She fucked up right now."

"Man fuck. This was not the shit I was trying to be on today." I spat as I stood from my seat and dropped a twenty on the table to cover my breakfast. Next, I snatched the paper from Roc with Niema's hospital room number on it and I went upstairs to call her.

The whole elevator ride back up to my room, I just felt numb. Hearing that shorty didn't have a heartbeat was fucking with me deep. I know I wasn't thrilled about having a baby with Niema and all, but damn. I knew how thrilled she was and to know what she was about to deal with had me by the chest.

I got in my room and made me a drink and then swallowed whatever it was I was feeling and dialed the number directly to Niema's room in the hospital. The phone rung about four times before she finally picked up and I could immediately hear not only the pain in her voice, but the sadness and it made me feel like a whole piece of shit. I almost hung up on her before I spoke. Not because I didn't care, but because I felt like shit.

But after she said Hello the third time I went on and spoke up. I had to be a man about this shit."

"How you feeling Ema?"

"Motherfucka… You really have some nerve."

"Niema please don't start this shit. Roc told you had the baby and I'm just trying to check up on y'all and…"

"Check up on us? My motherfucking son is dead and you calling to check up on us!."

"Niema chill. It's not like that. If I could be there with you then I would be and you know it."

"I don't know shit Juan! I don't know shit but you left me and my son and…" She started to sob uncontrollably and the shit broke me inside. "And now I have nobody."

"It's okay Ema. Look, let me call you back in a little bit, I need to take care of something." I lied because I needed to get off the phone with her. Hearing her like this was crushing me, especially knowing it was nothing I could do to help ease her pain at this point.

"That's the fucking problem Juan! You always need to take care of any motherfucking thing except for me! Im fucking falling apart here! My son… OUR MOTHERFUCKING SON IS NOT ALIVE NIGGA!

"The way I heard her break down after saying that, I couldn't do shit but hang up. I felt like shit for the way I had left her behind and how I couldn't be there with her while she went through this. I just sat there for a while not knowing what to say or do for real.

The rest of the trip, I wasn't shit for real. I kinda just stayed in my room trying to make sense of my life and the shit that was happening in it. Here I was a nigga with more money than I could ever spend in this lifetime, but I was so unhappy. My heart was broken by two bitches that I tried to give the world to and I didn't know why on either side. I had a daughter I loved with my whole heart that I didn't know when I would ever see again, and a son that I would never meet because his life ended before it even got started. Then the one chick I know wanted nothing more than to love me forever, I couldn't see myself with. I was fucked up and no amount of money could fix that shit. Here I was on a vacation in paradise and I had not a smile to place on my face. I didn't understand why my life had to be like this. But it was, what it was.

We spent a few more days in Brazil and for real on my part it was wasted money because I aint do shit but sit up in my room like my name was Brandy Norwood or some shit. When we left, I headed back to Panama where I was slated to live out my days for the time being. Each day even surrounded by all I had was pure unmitigated torcher on a whole different level.

By the time the summer had rolled around, Mikey ass pleaded because he didn't want to fuck around and blow trial. I mean seriously, it was like no way he was gonna walk on that shit. He spazzed and let that thang fly in front of what motherfuckas said looked like the whole Howard University community. Tia got them to drop the attempted murder charges and he pleaded to the weapons charges and took a easy 5 to 10. It may not sound like an easy bid BUT considering he was facing 15 to 30 initially, that five year minimum was gonna be a cake walk for him.

While he was tied down on this shit, Roc and I worked the business because even though they had my man in a cage, it was still money to be made hand over fist. I now had it set up where

Roc and my cousin Manuel on Pops side would meet me in Panama when it was time to flood them streets. Beforehand they had to get at me with them numbers and I would head to the compound like two weeks before they touched and get that shit ready to go. By time they got to Panama they could literally fly in and right back out cause the shit was ready to go, but since I was over that bitch by myself, they usually stayed a few days and we would hang and party and shit like that. Manuel was holding down the West and Roc was holding down the East. Pops wasn't 100% cool on Manuel's promotion but since Mikey and I both were out of commission for the moment, he had no choice but to accept it.

When school let out in Maryland for the summer I sent for my daughter. When her and my moms and the sisters stepped off the plane I was elated. I missed the ladies in my life like a motherfucka, and although we talked constantly, that shit wasn't nothing like being able to kiss your mother on her forehead or lay back and read and book to your baby girl. My mother and sisters stayed for a week before heading back to the states and although they were gone, I had TiTi for a few more weeks and that kept a nigga spirit up. While Sissy and her crew were there *they gave me the 3rd degree about how shit went down with Niema and I. Apparently, after our son died, she had him shipped back to DC where she buried him next to her father. She had been back since then and from what they were saying, she was having a real hard time accepting how things ended between us on top of our son passing. My mother said she tried to explain to her as simply as possible why I just disappeared, but she wasn't hearing nothing. I can't lie, a few times after they left, even before they came, I thought about her. I even picked up the phone a time or two to call her but thought better of it. I had taken shorty through enough and now I just wanted to give her the space she needed to heal from the hurt I brought in her life.*

By Oy time October rolled around, I found myself having to switch shit up again. Tia had gotten word that Roc name had popped up in a federal investigation, so he had to get low. It only made sense that he came to Panama with me. Since we both were not fucking with the States at the moment, we put together a little parlay in Panama for the big spenders we had on the East. It was about ten of them total. They came out and I set them up nice for the weekend. Them niggas ate good, fucked good and enjoyed the sunshine for two days then we got down to business. Them niggas had made millions over the years fucking with us, so if they wanted to keep fucking with us, they needed to buy planes. That was my word. Buy a plane and come get your own shit. Of course since I was eliminating the risk that came with transporting that shit, I was giving them a price break. Of the ten that came only three wasn't fucking with it and sadly for them, they aint make it back home. I guess they had tricked off the money they was making or whatever the case may be BUT since we was cutting business ties I couldn't send them niggas back knowing how we was about to start moving. Keep in mind my right-hand's name was sitting in a folder in some suit downtown office, so I wasn't leaving nothing to chance. The seven that went home, went home with the name of my nigga who could get them a plane and the plan for how we would do shit moving forward.

The next few months breezed by and then Christmas rolled up. In traditional fashion, my family and I rolled with Ian for his annual trip. We all headed to Iceland and while it was dope as shit, it wasn't the same without my little brother in the mix. Shane was still in the picture because she was holding him down finally as his wife. It took for him to have to sit his ass down behind a wall for him to say I do and make an honest woman out of her, but he did it and everybody was thrilled about it. It was good seeing some reminders of home, but I missed my wild ass little brother like nobody business.

While we were Iceland seeing a whole different side of the world, Pops got a call that Karma had struck back in DC. Magdelena and two of her homegirls had been found murdered in Magdelana's apartment. We didn't get the full details until we got back to Panama which is where Pop's brother, Magdelena's father, lived as well. Somebody had done my cousin dirty. They shot her friends but beat her literally to death. I knew then it was personal and figured Bell had something to do with it because who knew what type of shit he had her all caught up in. Before I could put in a call to my peoples to see if they were hearing anything in the streets about whatever went down with my cousin, Tia was hitting me up to let me know the same night Maggie met her demise, Public Enemy Number One did as well. I knew then whatever happened to my cousin had some shit to do with his ass as well.

I was fucked up that she died, even though she tried to throw me in a trick bag, she was still family. Apparently, Bell and his peoples got killed in a rinky dink motel either trying to sell or trying to buy some coke. I figure whoever got to him decided to get her ass too. Being that they did her so dirty I'm guessing whoever did them in was people her scandalous ass put on to him. She probably just wasn't expecting to die as well. Now that I knew the only motherfuckas that could connect me and Penny were gone on to be with their lord, I relaxed a bit. After we buried Maggy I spoke to Pops about me heading back to the States, but her shot that down immediately. I was semi blown because his point was valid. It was too soon point blank. These motherfuckas had just been killed and if I popped up ASAP they would label my dumb ass the prime suspect. Then there was still the whole fact that Roc name came up in an investigation about some other shit. So I didn't protest pops decision. I did however keep checking in with my people who had their feet on the ground in DC and more and more about the behind the scenes of Maggy and that bitch nigga death was coming out. I wasn't sure who they had played with but obviously they were the wrong motherfuckas to try because it sounded like a whole hit squad went after their asses.

Maggy was found with two other bitches and his bitch ass was found with three other dudes. Then the word on the street was this nigga was fucking with a white boy out Bethesda who turned up dead in the parking lot of a salon he and Bell co owned and a rack of bodies were found inside. The inside bodies all seemed to just be folks who were at the wrong place at the wrong time. I can't front, I was jive impressed by the way them folks hit his operation from all angels and deaded that shit. It was made clear that the taxation days in D.C were over. It was all kinds of rumors in the street with niggas claiming they was behind that shit, but I knew that was bogus. I learned a long time ago the nigga screaming 'I DID THAT SHIT!' was 9 times out of 10 lying and clout chasing. I was taught to keep my eyes on the motherfuckas who said nothing. And what I found to be interesting is niggas was saying that BJ was tight lipped all the way around about the situation.

Word on the street was that when other niggas discussed Bell in the days following, he would fall back from the convo and eventually excuse himself. Roc kept saying he could see him doing that shit, but I didn't know for sure. I didnt get hella suspicious not even a month later when he reached out to Roc to up his order. This nigga came through wanting a whole 1500 thangs. I needed a few days to sleep on that one because shit wasn't adding up. This nigga like doubled up on what he was getting to last him three months over night. Roc kept saying he trusted him and while he had never done no wild shit that would make me think he was one I had to really watch, the come up he was asking for was massive. I told him I would fuck with him and to come through. I also told him since he was coming for so much, I'd drop his price to 12 a piece. I set it up for him to come through for the pickup, but I had more on my mind than just hitting this nigga off and it being that. BJ had been cool but now I felt like I needed to really sit down and get to know the nigga I was fucking with because he seemed to be the new power that be in DC. No other niggas we was fucking with, even out West was making these kind of moves and now I felt it was my duty to find out how he was doing so.

When they landed at the private airport, I sent a car to pick them up and we met them at the apartment I had for business meetings and shit because although these niggas was on my turf, they would NEVER know where I laid my head. I set them niggas up with company for the night and sent word that I was coming through the next morning because I wanted to holla at BJ before he got his shit and was out. When we got to the apartment these niggas were up and dressed. I thought they would've been chilling but that wasn't the case. Roc told me the night before that I should chill on my questioning of these niggas because technically, they aint owe me no type of explanation of why they was moving how they was about to start moving, and he was right. They weren't a part of my crew or no shit like that. I was the connect. His business was his business, like mine was my business so he could tell me get the fuck on with my line of questioning...

BUT...

We all know how that shit would've played out. I felt like BJ and I had developed a mutual respect over time in this business so we could have a conversation without nobody getting in their feelings, so I tried my hand."

"What's up big spender." I joked as I walked into the room where he and his man Kody were chilling.

"Aint shit." Bj responded while standing to dap up both Roc. "Shit I'm tryna get on your level my man."

"I feel you. I see you getting close huh? Do I need to be worried?" I half ass joked as we dapped up Koby.

"Hold up, where my man Shank?" Roc asked as we all got settled in our seats around the table.

"Oh, he good. He back home running the show." BJ informed us. "My man Koby ready to step out from under my wing so I brought him to speak to y'all personally on his thing."

"That's cool. But with that wall they loading you down with right now as we speak, why you just aint get that money?" I inquired.

"Cause that's spoken for. And besides, this nigga like a brother to me so I felt like he could benefit straight from the source."

"And on top of that, I'm about to step off and head down south." Koby tossed out there to clear up any suspicions that may have been forming in our heads.

"Oh so y'all motherfuckas tryna take over the whole U.S of Motherfucking A huh?" Roc joked, but I was feeling like it was some truth behind that shit.

"Respect. Respect." I shook Koby hand in congratulations for stepping out on his own. "Now you know we aint gonna take you on for no small shit right?"

"Of course not. I'm hip to how shit work. I wouldn't even waste your time on no lowball numbers."

"That's what I like to hear. So let's do this. You go holla at Roc about what you need and such because I jive needed to rap to BJ on the solo tip."

"I can dig it." Koby said as he stood up and followed Roc down the hall to the other room leaving BJ and I alone.

I could see the wheels in BJ head turning trying to figure out what I need to holla at him about. I took my time approaching the conversation because I wanted to be sure I didn't come off as threatening and shit. I wanted answers... not a reason to kill this nigga. So I gave my thoughts a moment to marinate before I jumped straight into what was on my mind. "So what's really good BJ?"

"What you talking about? Aye look, I hope it wasn't no problem with me bringing Koby with me to holla at y'all personally."

"Oh nah, y'all good on that. Koby cool peoples. Trust me if it was a problem y'all would've found out as soon as y'all stepped off that plane."

"I can dig it." He replied and I could see in his eyes he wasn't feeling the threat I had just spoke on his life in so many words. "So what's up?" He asked, I guess trying to hide his agitation with me.

"You did that shit didn't you?" I jumped straight into it. I was smiling when I tossed that accusation in his lap because I didn't want him to think it was no beef and shit behind a nigga feeding Bell all that lead.

"What shit?" He asked me with confusion etched all over his face. But I was hip to niggas playing the role, so I wasn't letting up.

"My man Bell." I offered him the clarity he claimed to be looking for. "Look nigga, this me and you speaking."

"I know that, but on some real shit that wasn't my work."

"Come on BJ." I persisted. "Although I'm a whole ocean away, I still got boots on the ground and ears to the pavement. And the streets are putting you in the mix. They say you slated to be the new King of DC. I'm just trying to figure out if I'm sitting in the presence of royalty my nigga." I threw up my hands in mock surrender.

"I hear you my man, but whoever giving you your info giving you that shit wrong." He spoke with a level of seriousness that let me know he really wasn't fucking around. "I aint gonna say my pockets aint been heavier since the bitch nigga met his demise, but that shit was not me. I was actually in A.C when it went down and got the word when I touched down like everybody else."

"You serious BJ."

"On everything my nigga."

"So it wasn't none of your people either? Cause I don't need to tell you how many times I done been on the other side of the world and had a nigga whole head opened up."

"I can't even imagine my nigga. But like I said my hands clean on this shit."

"Alright. I hear you." I decided to let it go because either this nigga was telling the truth, the whole truth and nothing but the truth or he was the king of poker faces. "Just know I would love to shake the man hand who cleared that nigga out of all our lives cause his ass was costly."

"I feel you." BJ says as he mentally exits the conversation. "So, you coming back to the states now?" He changed the narrative just a little too fast for me which made it clear BJ knew more than what he was letting on.

"Nah not yet. Shit, a nigga in paradise as you see."

"I can dig it. Shit I'd love to trade the concrete jungle for some fly ass shit like this."

"You done started thinking about your retirement?"

"I got a couple more years on the streets. Shit I got a whole family that depend on me."

"I feel you. But look, let me ask you this, who is your underboss? That nigga Shank?" I was trying to hold my composure, but it was something about that nigga I aint fuck with.

BJ started laughing immediately. "He always said you aint fuck with him."

"He a smart nigga. Truthfully speaking it's something in that nigga eyes that rub me the wrong way. And he talks too much."

"Man listen…"

"If it wasn't for you, I would've been shot that nigga back in the day."

"So that's why you ask about who up under me. Let me guess you wouldn't fuck with him if something happened to me."

"Without question." I offered honestly without hesitation.

"Don't even worry about that. I got somebody in place to step up if shit ever went left on my end."

"Yeah. Who's that?"

"I'm still around so it doesn't matter. Just know, she as thorough as they come my nigga."

"She?" He had my full attention now.

"Oh yeah." This nigga was smiling and winked at me. I was one hundred percent confused.

"So you'd give the game to a bitch?"

"Let me be the one to tell you, shorty earned her stripes. So If I ever step down or God forbid fall, Queen got me."

"That's her name huh? What she your shorty."

"With all due respect…"

"Say nomore. I feel you." I retreated on the conversation because I could see we were at a crossroads where I would more than likely have to kill this nigga if I pressed on. I offered him dap to signal that I respected the end of the conversation.

I sat there with BJ and kicked it about nothing really until Roc and Koby got finish talking. I think our conversation had us both in our own thoughts. I aint know who this Queen bitch was, but I had all intentions of finding out ASAP. His whole need to keep her secret had me wanting to know who the bitch was cause I aint know any bitches out DC that was thorough enough to have a nigga be willing to hand them the whole game if he fell. Either this bitch was the TRUTH, or her pussy was out of this world and had this nigga confused. Either way, I jive needed to know who this bitch was.

By time their plane lifted off the next day, I was already hollering at my peoples to find out about a bitch that ran with BJ name Queen… as well as to keep eyes on this nigga. He had just picked up a game changing shipment so if this bitch was the person he was planning to hand the game to, now would be the time he would be seen fucking with her more than likely. A whole month went by and I was convinced that BJ was lying and this bitch did not exist. From what my peoples was telling me, wasn't no bitches on the set but the same ole bitches from back in the day and I knew them bitches. Wasn't NONE of them the type a nigga would give the game to. I was ready to have them niggas follow him home but then Roc was like let that shit go. He was right. BJ hadn't violated so it wasn't cool to violate that nigga privacy. On the strength of Roc, I let that shit go and went back to living life. It still crossed my mind from time to time though and I couldn't pinpoint why, it was like I just really wanted to know who this bitch was for some reason.

Then I got the call that validated why I had been wondering about the bitch I didn't even know for quite a while.

THE CUFFS WENT CLINK-CLINK

BJ got knocked, and from what the streets was saying, he wasn't coming home AT ALL. The word was going around that he went to meet a nigga with fifty bricks on him and got jammed up. At first, I was like maybe it was a routine traffic stop until Roc was giving me the word that he was getting from back home saying they had them big boys shut down a whole interstate to get him. I know half of what the streets be saying is bullshit so I had Tia pull his file and sure enough that's what happened. It just said they had a tip and the tip panned out and in the end my man was left holding the bag on fifty bricks and a whole half dozen bodies. I was thrown for a loop because as precise as I had known BJ to move, to be out here pissing in the wind with a dirty gun and a life sentence in weight was crazy.

I had my sister keeping her ears to the ground on this one because again, this nigga was one of my biggest spenders PERIOD and I needed to know what type of moves he was making. Roc kept screaming his man wasn't like that, but like I kept telling him, niggas change up quick when they are looking at football numbers.

When Tia came back about a week later and told me he waived counsel and took a deal, that he'd eat the weight in exchange for them dropping the bodies because he had never seen that gun in his life, I knew then that he really was set up and the fucked up thing was he knew who did it. I had learned from my own past situations that bitches were treacherous, and I was *convinced my man had fallen victim to that shit. I thought it was odd as fuck how as soon as he started making these power moves, my man find himself in cuffs. Like the whole time he had been up in the mix he's never got so much as a traffic ticket because like myself and the other niggas around me, we were careful. Only place that seemed to be our downfall was trusting these bitches. It always seemed to bite us in the ass in the end.*

With that I decided I was gonna wait a few months and see if anything changed on his stance because at any moment this nigga could get to working with them peoples once the shock that his bitch set him up wore off and he felt the weight of them years on his neck. The minute he asked for an attorney I was gonna sic Tia on him to find out where this nigga head was at because while I got he was Roc man from way back, my freedom outweighed all that shit so I wasn't trying to hear nothing. Then April of 1997 rolled through and changed everything for a nigga."

Chapter Two

In the month and half that BJ had been down nothing with him had changed as far as his stance on his case. He wasn't asking for no lawyer and hadn't hired one and was just waiting for them people to sign off on his years. I was starting to relax a bit until Roc got word that Koby wouldn't be making anymore buys with us after all. This nigga suitcase barely stopped rocking down in Dallas before niggas took his head all the motherfucking way off and walked with it. Roc was in his chest about that shit and ready to go to war but like I told him wasn't nothing happening. True Koby was cool peoples from what I knew of him, but he wasn't OUR peoples. So wasn't no hot ones being fired in his honor.

I knew Roc wasn't feeling my position because again he knew these niggas since kindergarten. So, I understood but at the same time this wasn't our beef. I also found out that nobody had seen BJ's right-hand Shank since the day this nigga got caught up. I guess BJ was on to something when he said this bitch was certified *because it seemed like she had cleared the chess board on them niggas and disappeared in the wind with all that coke the nigga had just copped. This was exactly why I didn't fuck around with consignment niggas anymore. When somebody opens up your motherfucking chest and clear out the stash, I still need my money. This shit is why I had always been adamant about fucking with niggas who had straight cash for what they wanted. This weeded out the niggas looking to flip their girl taxes or just wanting to stunt saying he in the street. And I guess that's why for the most part, my life on the business side had been stress free, because I never had to worry about a nigga owing me. It kept shit simple, and that's how I liked things to be.*

However, motherfuckas loved to interrupt my simplicity.

I had started to date again at this point Nothing serious like how shit was moving in my life before but keeping it real a nigga had needs and Panama had some of the finest bitches on earth roaming around. So I figured why not. Roc and I had invited these bitches we had been talking to over for the evening. I had my private chef whip us up some food and we were chilling, drinking good and playing board games getting to know each other. Really just passing the time until we were ready to know what these bitches fuck faces were hitting on. Then my phone rung and shit changed.

I started not to answer, but then I saw it was Anna Maria, I figured I better take it because I wasn't expecting nobody coming in with BJ being locked up. I answered the phone and she told me she had a bitch name Queen on the line. I damn near jumped through the roof knowing this shady bitch had surfaced. I told her go on and schedule her in BJ slot. It killed me to keep quiet that whole night about who had called and what they wanted, but I didn't want to take away from our company so I pushed that little gem to the back of my mind and focused on shoving dick in every hole the bitch I was kicking it with had. The next morning after we fed them breakfast, I had a car take them home. While Roc and I sat at the table, him reading the paper and me half ass watching CNN, I decided to go ahead and fill him in on what was to come.

"So, remember that call I got last night. I'll give you a million dollars if you could guess who it was." I laughed fucking with him.

"Man will you shut the fuck up with your betting ass and just tell me."

"Your peoples, peoples."

"Who is that?" He quizzed in confusion.

"The bitch we been looking for that fuck with BJ. She called yesterday to book her trip my nigga."

"Get the fuck outta here."

"Cousin, I'm dead ass serious."

"So you think he done changed his stance?"

"You know I got Tia on it checking in to see. I called her ass before I even opened my eyes good this morning."

"I bet he still standing on his time. But this lil sneaky bitch probably feeling like the coast might be clear for her to come out now."

"That's what I was thinking."

"I wish I could speak to that nigga before."

"Well I've already decided this bitch gotta go as soon as she gets here."

"I figured you would say that."

"I mean, it aint like she knows us BUT we already see how she playing out in these streets and I aint about to break bread with no scandalous ass hoe like that."

"I can dig it my nigga. When is she coming?"

"In two days my nigga." I informed him giddy as fuck.

"Damn nigga what you so hyped about?"

"I aint killed a motherfucka in awhile Roc. I'ma do this greedy bitch so dirty." I was rubbing my hands together in pure excitement and the whole nine.

"You a whole ass psychopath cousin." Roc laughed as he drank his coffee and went back to reading his paper.

"I dismissed Roc and his name calling and went on with my day. I worked out for a bit, talked to my daughter and my mom on the phone then just chilled for real. I was just counting down those two days when I got to meet the secret that had BJ sitting over in the jail right the fuck now.

On the day of her arrival, it seemed like time was moving at a fucking snail's pace. I was itching to kill this bitch that I had never met before. I knew she was scheduled to land around 6pm so I had a nice chauffeured 600 waiting on her, while Roc and I sat behind the tint of the chauffeured Suburban at the other side of the tarmac waiting ever so patiently. The driver had his instructions on where to take this bitch and whoever was with her and I couldn't wait. I had the table set up and ready for her ass. When BJ's plane started coming in for a landing, we just watched and waited as the ground crew got in position. As the door opened, Roc and I both had given our undivided attention to it, just to get a glimpse of this bitch who thought she was ready to play with the big boys."

"Yo, it's two of them bitches." Roc said with excitement while watching the two of them float down the steps.

"I'm not surprised she didn't come alone. Besides, scandalous hoes usually move in packs."

"They thick as shit from where I'm sitting."

My eyes almost bugged out of my head when I really focused in on the bitches using my long-range binoculars. I punched Roc hard as shit to grab his attention because for a second I thought the fucking weed had me hallucinating and shit. "My nigga, do you see who the fuck that is?"

"What? Two thick ass scandalous hoes that I'm thinking we should at least run through before them bitches end up on the table."

"That's fucking Keeli nigga! Look good! I'd know that shiesty bitch anywhere nigga!" I damn near shoved my binoculars against Roc eyes because it was clear his shits was not giving him the same view I had.

"Aye yo Rafiq, pull closer to them bitches. Not all the way up on them but where we can see better. Cause cousin I think you lunching right now."

"Yes Boss." Rafiq replied as he honored Roc's request.

"I'm telling you Roc, that's her. That's her sister that was on the boat with her that night when we linked back up and shit." I yelled while pointing at them as Rafiq drove us closer to where they were standing and waiting while their shit was being taken off the plane.

"I looked at Keeli and so much shit from our short time together made sense. I remember the night this bitch actually said to me that she was a drug dealer, joking and shit, but as we see she was being 100% authentic and my dumb ass was just so wrapped up in the way she rode a nigga dick I couldn't see it. Now it all made sense. How she stayed laced and was NEVER trying to be in my pockets. This bitch was fucking round in the streets heavy.

Now I was wondering about her connection to BJ, I mean it had to be something deep for him to give this bitch the game. It also made sense why Bell was out here in these streets looking for her. I sat there and watched her in pure silence and slight awe at how crafty her ass had been. She was out here with all kinds of alias, playing me,Bell, the nigga Simm who felt the need to call me back and BJ. Sissy told me from the moment she met her that Keeli was scandalous. I don't think either of us had a clue of how she got the fuck down.

I sat there and stared at her and while all the pieces of the puzzle were trying to finally link up and make sense in my head, my heart… a nigga heart had a mind of its own.

My chest was so warm, and I could feel the shit in my stomach just watching her. She was standing there smiling and talking with her peoples and she just had this energy about her that I couldn't explain. She looked damn good though, she definitely had got a little thicker since the time when I used to beat that box. Her black ass was still stunning, and she carried herself like she truly belonged in the position she was sitting in.

The original plan was to have their driver take them to the spot and we were gonna roll up and dismantle these bitches, but once I laid eyes on her, I had to call an audible. I needed answers. Real live answers from everybody involved in this shit. And not the kind of answers motherfuckas give when they strapped down to a table getting ready to have their body parts cut off limb by limb. I wanted the truth. I real live loved this bitch, even when I didn't want to love her whore ass nomore. Now I needed to know was any of it real for her, or was it all a means to get to the seat she was in now. I was still gonna kill that bitch. That shit I was 99.999999% sure of. But first I needed to know the things I needed to know.

I grabbed the car phone and called their driver just as they climbed into the backseat and told him plans had changed and to take their ass to the apartment to chill and let them know he would be there in the morning to pick them up for breakfast. As soon as I hung up, Roc goofy ass was all smiles."

"I see you had a change of heart my nigga. I told you if it was meant to be the universe would bring her back your way."

"Nigga fuck the universe. This ho played with me. I'm just giving her an extra day to live while I check into some shit, but tomorrow morning I can promise you I put a bullet in her fucking brains."

"Yeah alright. That shit sound slick, and if it was anybody else, I believe your cold ass would do it. But her..Nigga that bitch been your destiny. Y'all both just been too distracted to see it."

"I aint say shit else, I sat back in my seat while Rafiq drove us on out of the airport. I didn't know if Roc was on to something with what he was saying, but I needed answers about a

lot of shit before I killed her. The Benz they were riding in was in front of us, and it was like all I could do was sit there and watch it knowing she was inside. I was wondering about what she was saying, what she was feeling. If she knew who I was. If any of it was real. Even when the car turned off headed to downtown where the apartment was and we kept straight on heading out to where my Estate was, I couldn't say shit. I just sat there stuck in my own head trying to make sense of it all.

As soon as we got back to the house, I called Tia. I needed her to drop everything and take her ass over to the Jail and visit with BJ immediately. I was usually adamant about keeping my connections to the street and my family as separate as possible, like niggas would never know Tia was my sister. But today I needed her to pull that nigga for a lawyer visit and then call me ASAP on her cell because I needed to speak to him. She cussed me out and gave me shit, but two hours after I called her, my cell was ringing and her and BJ was on the other end."

"What's good my nigga. How you holding up?" I asked BJ, just trying to break the ice, because at this point, I really didn't care how he was doing.

"I'm holding up. But what's this all about. I know you don't think I'm…"

"Man chill and listen. I got a question for you right quick. Do you know who jammed you up?"

"Hell yeah I know who."

"And who was that?"

"You know how they always say don't let your right hand know what your left is doing?"

"You positive on that B?" I questioned because it was clear we weren't reading from the same book.

"One hundred percent. Why you asking though?"

"Cause you know he aint been around since that shit happened to you. Motherfuckas thinking he may have got caught up in the twist and somebody else might be behind all y'all forced retirements."

"Nah, I'm positive that nigga aint get caught up in no twist. That nigga was the twist."

"Okay, so let me ask you this. The bitch you were telling me about when we sat down. What's your relationship to her?'

"Listen man, I'm telling you she aint have shit to do with what I'm going through. That shit was all on him." I could hear the irritation rising in his voice.

"You trust her like that? What that's your bitch or something?" I pressed on.

"Fuck no man."

"So who is she to you?"

"Do it even matter at this point?"

"Yeah it does." I stood firm letting him know I wasn't asking him to tell me about her no more... I was demanding.

"Did she reach out to you?"

"Yeah she did. But with the shit I'm hearing in the streets and the vibe I got I need to know the extent of y'all relationship, because you are vouching so hard for her and I need to know exactly why. The pussy can't be that good my nigga."

"Yo B, we aint never had a motherfucking problem before, and I want to keep it that way. I fucks with you and appreciate everything you've done for me, but don't disrespect my family like that again. On some G shit, that's not gonna be tolerated."

It was clear I had struck a nerve with my line of questioning. I took a minute before I responded because I was trying to calm myself. If I aint know any better, I would've believed the nigga just threatened me. I counted down backwards from ten before I spoke again. "Listen, don't get all caught up in your chest about some shorty on the squad. I'm trying to find a reason to override the vibes this broad is giving me and the shit they saying about her out in the street, and still fuck with her. I'm telling you they say her hands all in the mix."

"Listen B. I'm not sure what your angel is right now but I'm telling you that's bullshit. Shorty aint nobody on the squad. Shorty is my blood. If you are feeling some type of way and you aint trying to fuck with her off your vibe, I respect that. Just know that's been your biggest spender for years. That wall I had you build, that was for her. Not me. I kept her in the cut because that's family and it's my job to protect her."

"Yeah." I heard his little soliloquy, but I wasn't trying to hear that shit. "So just tell me this, is Keeli even really her name?"

"How the fuck you know her government Slim?" I could hear the confusion falling off this nigga voice.

"It's a long story my nigga. One I don't even think you would believe if I told you."

"Man don't tell me you used to fuck with her or no shit like that."

"Alright, I wont tell you then."

"Come on man. You can't be serious."

"Look, I'ma let you go but just answer me this one thing. Did she ever marry that nigga Simm?"

"Get the fuck outta here." BJ laughed. "I would've put a bullet in her head myself had she married that clown ass nigga. That shit was a wrap years ago. Nigga was nothing but a means to end."

"Yeah." I filled the space with a lone yeah because I didn't know what else to say. Nothing had been as it seemed.

"Listen man. I don't know what you and her have been through, but I can tell it's jive serious considering you had your peoples come all the way over here to see me so we can speak. I don't know the logistics of y'all shit because while her ass is like a little sister to me, her love life aint shit we ever discussed unless it was a problem and she needed me to step in. But everything I said about her when we spoke before stands. She official. She learned from me. And that shit you was asking me about. The shit you kept tryna get me to sign my name on with them peoples. That's the hand you wanna shake right there."

"Get the fuck outta here!" I shouted in disbelief.

"I'm telling you no lies."

"Wow. She really had me fooled and… you know what, I'ma have my peoples keep your shit filled up and…"

"Listen B, I could feel the shift in your voice just now. And I know Ke grown, but that's still my baby. If y'all gonna be on some romance shit, please just take care of her."

"I got you my nigga."

"Alright. Peace."

"Peace."

We hung up the phone and I just sat there while everything was swirling around in my head. Roc had been listening to the whole conversation and he was just as stuck as I was. I never would've thought the bitch who stole my heart was the motherfucking female King in them streets.

That night, I think I barely slept an hour. I just laid in my bed and over analyzed every conversation we had ever had. I was trying to figure out how I didn't see that shit in her. How was I not able to connect the dots before now. I even called Tia back and woke her ass up out her sleep when it hit me that they knew each other before I introduced them. It was like pulling teeth to get Tia to tell me how she knew Keeli ass. She claimed she was the go-between for somebody on a case she worked before but now I aint believe her knowing this bitch had just purchased 1200 kilos of coke from me a few months ago and was now here to buy more. I felt so stupid knowing I had brought a whole ring and was ready to ask shorty to be my wife, and it turns out I didn't even know her ass at all.

The next morning, I was dressed before the sun even came up all the way. I couldn't wait to see her face when she saw mine. I couldn't wait to get to the bottom of all the shit I had questions about that had transpired. When I got the call that they had been picked up, my nerves were fucking with me heavy. Me and this woman hadn't stood in the same space since the night she showed up at my house to profess her undying love for me. So many times since that night I wished I could rewind shit to our meet up and the motel. I wished she would have spoken her truth then about how she felt about me. I would've gone home and put Niema ass out right then and got shit right with her. So much shit that transpired after that night probably would've been avoided had she spoke her truth before then about being in love with me.

There was a part of me that question if the love we said we felt for each other was real considering it was built on lies on both of our part. Hell, I wasn't honest with her about who I was in these streets either. But while I lied about who I was, I never lied about how I felt about her. I legit wanted to marry shorty… her lies and all. I was ready and then shit just rolled down hill starting with that phone call from her so-called man.

When their car pulled up in my driveway, I sat in front of the cameras in my surveillance room and just studied her face. She was still as beautiful as the day I met her ass up in Georgetown. I can't even fake, my dick got brick damn near instantly watching her walk from the car inside the house. Once Maria took them outside where we would be meeting by the pool, I closed my eyes and said a prayer that everything worked out the way it was supposed to. With that, I left the surveillance room and headed down to stand face to face with the one that got away. Maria and I made our way out to the pool area where they were sitting at and came in on the ass end of a toast that gave me my first glimpse into the real Keeli."

Keeli raises her glass for a toast. "To getting money."

"For the rest of our lives." Ciaira counters as they clink glasses and begin to drink.

"Maria and I stepped into their view just as they started to drink their mimosa. You would've thought she had seen a ghost as big as her eyes got and then she spit the whole fucking drink on her girl. It was hard as shit to stifle my laugh, but it was clear that she was just as surprised about who I was, as I was as to who she was."

"I'm so sorry Ci." Keeli half ass pleaded with her folks, but she never took her eyes off me the whole time.

"Oh my God. This shit is crazy." Ciaira was pissed, but she was burning a hole in me as well.

"Maria, take her inside and get her cleaned up." I said still trying to hold back my laugh.

"Yes sir. Ms. Princess, please come with me."

Maria and Ciara left and headed back in the house so she could get cleaned up and me and Keeli just stood there in this crazy ass stare off. I had just been ready to laugh a minute ago, but the way she looked at me. It fucked with me. I had hurt this girl and even though she was out here making major moves you could clearly see that shit in her eyes. I didn't know what to do or say at this moment. All that fly shit I had been thinking about earlier went slam out the window and I was just stuck taking her in while a member of my service staff cleaned up the mess she made. As soon as he walked away, my dumb ass tried to lighten to mood by offering her an olive branch by way of a smile, and all hell broke loose.

"I guess you are just as surprised to see me as I was to see you step off that plane last night. Please sit down." I motioned to the table as I pulled out her chair. She sat in it but it was clear she wasn't too thrilled about it. I sat next to her and placed my hand on top of hers, because I just needed to touch her at this point. But she wouldn't even look at me. She just stared out over the infinity pool to some far off place. I had so much I wanted to say, but I could feel the tension coming from her and didn't want to make this shit worse than what it was. So I gave her the silence she was silently requesting, but found victory in her not snatching he hand the fuck away from mine immediately. It took about 5 whole uncomfortable minutes that felt like a fucking lifetime before she finally spoke.

"I'm confused. You told me you were an investor."

"And you told me you were a preschool teacher." I chuckled trying to get her to see we were both sitting here with dirty hands.

"I guess we both lied." Her voice was so small and filled with so much hurt and confusion that it hurt me.

"That's the way it looks." My tone was reflective of hers. "Who would've ever thought that my biggest customer in the states was the one who got away."

"You mean the one you PUSHED away." She snapped at me.

"Nah, you pushed yourself away with your little live in boyfriend and shit."

"What about you and that bitch!! The fucking Queen of fake ass Fendi!"

"Why are you yelling? I'm right here."I snapped because she annoyed the shit out of me quick bringing up Niema for a number of reasons. Then her tone just blew me. I was trying with her ass and she just started yelling and shit.

"I'm not yelling." She was trying hard to hold her composure, but the damage was done.

"Anyway, that was nothing."

"I couldn't tell."

"Well that shit is neither here nor there." I was trying to steer the conversation away from our rocky past. "You look good." I complimented her genuinely because she did look damn good.

"I always do." She snapped back giving me her ass to kiss with her facial espression.
"You know what, maybe today is not such a good day to talk business with you. You seem a little emotional." I regretted saying that shit as soon as the words echoed in my head.

"Emotional!" She repeated in disbelief. "Emotional! Motherfucka is you serious!" She finally flew off the deep end. "I tell you that I'm in love with you and then I find out you got some stank ass bitch up in your spot with you, fucking that ho!"

"You drove me to her!!" I yelled in her face from out of nowhere. Before I knew she had grabbed her homegirl drink that she left on the table and threw that motherfucka in my face. I swear on all my kids it took everything in me not to drag her ass to the pool and hold her the fuck under water until she just stopped breathing.

"Go to hell!" She yelled at me as she got up and stormed back in my house leaving me sitting at the table covered in a drink and alone. About two minutes later her girl came running back outside like the fucking house was on fire or something. She walked over to me and it was clear to see she was pissed but I didn't even give a fuck. Keeli ass had no idea how close I was to ending her fucking life not even twenty-four hours ago, so for her to give me all that ass to kiss when I was doing her ass a favor by just letting her fucking live, that was too much.

"So you really not gonna stop her?" Ciaira snapped at me.

"Hell no! That's what her ass want! She lookin for somebody to chase her and shit and I aint the motherfucka for that!" I started to pace to calm myself down because she really had me about to boil the fuck over playing these dumb ass game. After a minute or two I pulled it together when I realized her girl was still standing there looking at me like I had her completely fucked up at this point. I took a deep breath and blew out my frustrations before I walked back over to her and grabbed her hand gently and looked into her eyes.

"Look, let her go back to the apartment and blow off some steam. In an hour or two, we'll go over and talk to her. But right now, let's have some breakfast." I asked as calmly as I could. She didn't protest, she just threw her hands up in surrender and mumbled something about how we both were getting the fuck on her nerves and then she went and sat down at the table.

Ciaira and I ate in silence. I'm not sure what was on her brain, but I was still mentally digesting all the shit that was coming to light about Keeli, so I aint have too much to say about nothing. Things kinda perked up a bit when Roc finally came outside to join us. "Good Morning." He said while looking at Ciaria and I could already tell this nigga was plotting on her ass.

"Good Morning." She offered back with a kind smile.

"Where my girl go?" He asked as he sat down and removed the cover from his breakfast tray.

"Your man ran her off." Ciaira offered with an eye roll that was so hood I felt like she wanted to fight my ass.

"Listen, you know your girl tripping. She rolled out on us and right now I'm just giving her space to calm down before we go check on her."

"You gonna go get your woman huh man." Roc jokes as a Segway into the conversation I wanted to have with Ciaira.

"Man, we all know that girl aint thinking about my ass. I been off her radar."

"That's cause you chose to be nigga." Ciaira immediately snapped in Keeli's defense.

"How you figure shorty?"

"Look, that's my sister so we not gonna act like I don't know the ins and outs of what y'all had back then. Juan, you broke her fucking heart and for a while her whole spirit with that fuck shit that went down at your house that night. My girl was 100% all in with you, so much so she humbled herself and came to you to tell you how she felt when she felt shit wasn't hitting like it used to between y'all. And nigga you had a whole bitch there wearing your chain in sense. You lucky she aint shoot both of y'all cause she was really hurt."

"Listen, I fucked up, but Keeli aint have cleans hands during our shit either. Hence her ass being here now on the other side of the world trying to buy bricks from me without even knowing it was me."

"Nigga you told the same lie she did so kill that."

"That's true B." Roc dumb ass added.

"Okay, I can get why she lied about what she does for a living. But listen, I done had run ins with three niggas on her behalf that she was fucking with. So her love couldn't have been that strong if she was still rocking with other niggas. And in my defense I aint start rocking with Niema again until I found out about her and the nigga Simm, as well as the nigga Bell."

"Simm? Bell? Ciaira laughs. You gotta be fucking kidding me."

"Nah I'm dead ass. And now I find out she fucking with my nigga BJ. That's the whole reason she over here. But I'm sure you already know that."

"Well let me be the one to pump your breaks on her and BJ. That's MY man." Ciaira boasted with pride. "That's her fucking cousin. Her dad, and his mom slid out the same hole many years ago."

"Oh so you fuck with BJ?" Roc inquires.

"Yeah. That's the love of my life." Her tone softened as she spoke on him letting us know it was real.

"I can dig it. So how you holding up with all the shit that's going on?"

"Barely. But for him and our son I gotta stay strong. He'd only spazz the fuck out on me if he thought I was out here breaking down." She chuckles.

"Yeah he probably would." Roc chuckles with her. "Well me and B been tight since like kindergarten and shit. I'm still fucked up he got caught out here slipping like that."

"Yeah that's what they say. But I know, and I'm damn sure y'all know too that he got set up."

"So you believe Shank had a hand in that?" I asked coming out my own thoughts.

"I aint no fool Juan. Shank greasy ass hands was all over that. Why? I'm not sure. But BJ told me everything. I was his sounding board cause we all know these streets is stressful and everybody needs an outlet. Somebody they can talk to about the shit they can't talk to nobody else about."

"True shit." Roc cosigned and I could tell he was digging her vibe even though she was spoken for by his man from way way back.

"And the nigga he was meeting up with the night the shit went down, was solely off the strength of Shank. Why he set him up, I couldn't tell you. But I do know he set him up."

"So why ole killa across town aint take his ass out yet?" I inquired. "Word on the street is she took out 65% of 5.D right after Christmas." I decided to fuck with her to see if it was truth to what BJ was trying to sell me about Keeli.

"I don't know what you talking about Sir." Ciaira fed me that lie with a look on her face that told it all then sipped her coffee in a way that said she was done talking about the shit.

"Y'all wild as shit." Roc laughs peeping the chess move homegirl had just made.

"Listen Juan, I'ma keep it G with you. You really hurt Keeli with that shit you pulled. I don't know why you pulled it, but you did. Now I know I would have to fight her ass if she ever found out I told you this, but… Keeli was pregnant when y'all broke up.

"Man get the fuck outta here." I waved her off not feeling like she was boosting the story.

"I'm so serious." Ciaira went in purse and pulled out a small photo book. "I don't leave home without pics of the people who mean the most to me."

She passed me the book and Roc goofy ass damn near fell over the chair to get over my shoulder to get a peek at her life she carried around in her purse.

The first picture we saw was her and BJ. The smiles on their face solidified what she was saying about being his woman. The smiles on their faces and the way he had her all wrapped in his arms screamed Shorty is mine. We saw a few pictures of her son with BJ and the three of them together. Then there were a few of what I'm guessing was her family and then there was one of her, Keeli and two other bitches. One I definitely remember from that night on the boat. They was like plain jane as fuck, so I'm guessing this was before they decided to get in the trenches. The next few pictures, you could tell they had they started getting money because everything about what they wore, to the way they styled their hair, to even the way they stood in the pictures screamed we getting it out here.

I couldn't help but smile getting this peek into the real Keeli. It was all starting to make sense to me now. I guess that's why I could never shake her ass. Shorty was the female version of me, and our shit was meant to be. As soon as I had the thought, my next thought was that I had to be tripping. I didn't even really know this girl… but I knew that I still loved her ass.

The last page of the book had me stuck in awe. It was two pictures. One of Keeli, CiCi and these two little shorties that I swear was like looking at TiTi as a baby all over again when she was little. Keeli had this smile on her face as she sat on the floor holding both babies in lap and CiCi stood behind her hanging on to her neck. Before I could even say anything, Roc was all on it."

"Damn my nigga. You couldn't deny them if you wanted to."

"Listen. I already feel like I just broke major code even showing you them, so please don't say anything to her about them until she tells you."

"How old are they?"

"They just turned one on March 9th."

Hearing that fucked me up. A year ago, on March 9th, while I was in Brazil celebrating my birthday, I had one son losing his life before it even started, but two more making their way into

*the world. My heart felt so conflicted at that
moment. I took the picture out her book and just
got up from the table and went in the house
leaving her and Roc outside to finish breakfast
without me. I needed time to myself to digest what
the fuck I had just found out. I had two sons out
there in the world. A part of me was ecstatic, but
another part was pissed that they had lived a
whole year without me, and her ass never even
tried to let me know what was what.
True enough I had been out the country for some
time, but she knew how to get in touch with both
Shane and Tia so she could've told me about my
sons.*

*I didn't know what the fuck Ciaira and Roc
had going on the rest of the day, but I was sure
he would keep her entertained while I tried to
wrap my head around the shit I was just served to
digest. There was a part of me that wanted to go
and grab her ass up and marry her
IMMEDIATELY so I would never have to worry
about being without her again in life. That was
the hopeless romantic in me. But there was
another part of me that wanted to take a machete
to her fucking limbs for not telling me about the
boys. I felt so slighted by that shit cause one thing
a nigga wasn't in this world was a deadbeat dad.
To know they had a whole year without me
fucked me up. I know Ciaira asked me not to say
shit til Keeli did, but it was killing me. I decided*

she had until tomorrow morning to tell me about my sons or they could take whatever rift to their situation they was gonna take because I was damn sure gonna say something to her about them.

Finally about 7pm, I emerged from my suite. I had taken another shower, faced a few J's and felt like her and I both had more than enough time to calm the fuck down from our earlier encounter. I came downstairs and found Roc and Ciaira sitting at the island in my kitchen playing tunk for shots. Roc was so full of shit, trying to get that girl drunk so her next move would be forgetting all that loyalty she claimed she had for BJ and parting them legs. I hated to rain on his program, but I needed to get to Keeli now. He had all day to try and talk this bitch out her panties, so it wasn't my fault. Besides, if I didn't end up leaving Keeli ass out in the jungle with her head missing, he would have more opportunities to talk shorty out her drawls.

On the ride to the apartment, I could tell that she was jive feeling Roc as well. She was filling me in on the afternoon they spent together after I ditched them as she said. You would've thought they had known each other their whole lives the way she spoke about him with a familiarity that made it clear that she was interested in him as well. I don't know if it was the loneliness of being without BJ these days or what but I could tell she was loving the attention Roc was giving her because she never stopped smiling as she talked about him and the time they shared. I just hoped that aint no shit pop off with BJ and this shit because even though he was locked up, niggas on the inside loved to try and assert their rights to some pussy on the outside.

I pushed any pending bloodshed out of my mind and focused on trying to find and maintain a calm space for my upcoming meeting with my baby mother. I chuckled to myself thinking about the fact that Roc had been on to something when he said Keeli was my destiny, we both was just too caught up to see it.

When we got to the apartment, she was in the livingroom sleeping like a baby on the sofa. I could see she had made herself at home cause she had put a dent in the bottle of Hennessy that was on the table and the leftover aroma of the weed she had smoked was still lingering. It was funny how in sync we were without even knowing it at the time. I sat down across from her on the loveseat while she slept and just took her in. She was beautiful, she was strong, she was complex, and I knew I wasn't gonna rest until she was mine all the way.

Ciaira stood in front of her to block my view of her as a way to get my attention because I was sitting there in a crazy man trance for a minute without even knowing it.

"I'm about to wake her up. Remember what you promised me Juan."

"I got you Ci. I promise." I said referring to our conversation before we came upstairs where she had me promise to be calm and not spazz on Keeli, and to let her be the one to tell me about the boys. I promised her all this shit and I was hoping I could keep that promise, but the ball was in her girl court for real. Because like I said earlier I had already decided she had until the sun rose the next day to tell me about our sons or I'd just fucking kill her and raise them myself.

Ciaira shook her drunk ass a few times before she opened her eyes wide as fuck and wiped the drool off her face with her arm. "What you wake me up for?" She snapped.

"Because y'all need to talk, so get up."

She looked over at me and it registered to her that I was sitting across from her, her eyes narrowed into these slits where shorty looked like she wanted to fucking spit on me. "I'm not leaving until you talk to me." I added to let her know this conversation was happening tonight no matter how she felt about the shit.

"I'ma go in the room and let y'all have some privacy." Ciaira said and walked out the living room. She went down the hall into her bedroom and closed the door leaving us with no one but ourselves.

Shorty immediately turned her back to me and kinda buried her face in the pillow she had been sleeping on. I had already peeped the water building up in her eyes. The last thing I wanted was to make her cry, so I got up and moved across the livingroom and sat next to her. "So you really not gonna talk to me?"

"No. I'm not."
"Look, stop acting like a fuckin brat." I spat because this shit was becoming annoying and again, I was trying to stay calm, but it was hard to do that with her grown ass acting like 4-year-old. "Sit up and act like a woman. Say what the fuck you feel." I demanded.

She sat up with a fire in her eyes that almost made me wished I had just let her stay in the sunken place she was in. "You wanna know what the fuck I feel! I fucking hate you right now!!" She yelled while getting up off the sofa. "I trusted you. I was in love with you and look what you did to me!!"

"You don't think I was hurt too! I call you because I can't fucking wait to get home to see you again and some bitch ass nigga come calling me talking about y'all live together and shit. How you think that shit made me fucking feel!

"It wasn't like that! Just like I told you before!"

"How was I supposed to know that!"

"You could've been up front with me about what you was feeling. You could've told me what happened, and I would've told you what was really going on."

"So what's really going on?"

"It don't matter now." She damn near whispered while wiping away her own tears.

I grabbed her and pulled her close to me because seeing her cry fucked me up. "It does matter to me." I assured her because I really did want to just put everything on the table and then figure out where we were going from that moment.

"I don't even know where to begin Juan."

"At the beginning is a good place to start."

"I don't know why Simm told you that, but shit wasn't like that between us. Simm was the nigga that helped me get on. He was my baby father best friend and CiCi Godfather or whatever. He gave me the money to cop my first bird looked out for me when me and my girls ran into trouble. But me and this nigga wasn't even engaged."

"Did y'all ever fuck with each other on that level?"

"I'm not gonna lie to you, we did mess around a few times. And for awhile we all stayed at his spot after my house got broken into but it was never on some let's get married type shit."

"So you aint never feel nothing for him Keeli? And don't lie."

"I'm done lying to you about shit. No I didn't. At least not like he felt for me. We was like family but after things took a turn he was pushing for an US and I was pushing for a me and you. This nigga backed me in a corner where I was almost assed out so that I would need him and that's why we ended up staying together for like three months, if it was even that. He did give me a wack ass proposal after he found out about you. And that same day he presented me with a ring and a shit load of questions about who you were and how I felt about you, I had BJ and his dudes come move me and my folks right up out his house."

"Oh yeah. So he questioned you about me?"

"Yes. I didn't know he had called you like a ho ass nigga. He claimed he had a P.I following me. He was so wack I believe he would've done that shit so I aint think nothing beyond it."

"And what you tell him about me?"

"I told him that I love you and more importantly, I was 100% IN LOVE with your ass."

"Is that right?" I found myself blushing at her revelation. "So if you were in a bind, why wouldn't you just come to me Keeli?"
"Because Juan. I wasn't trying to be in your pockets like that. I'm not some begging ass broad Juan. I make my own money. I've been out here getting it since late 93 and…"

"Speaking of that." I chuckled because it was crazy listening to her speak and knowing that she was really out here in the streets getting hers. "Why you aint just tell me what you was really on from the jump?"

"Nigga." She laughed like I had just told the biggest joke ever. "The same reasons you aint tell me what you was really on Mr. Real Estate investor."

"That was partially true though Keeli."

"But them houses you flipping aint how you making your living. That's how you clean it up. Don't play with me. And from the look of things, I'm guessing it's a lot more business in your portfolio because I know damn well BJ and I weren't the only people you was fucking with."

"Look at you all in my shit." I joked causing her to laugh.

"Nah I'm just saying I aint a dummy at all Juan."

"So you understand why I lied right?"

"Yeah about how you get your bread. But not about how you felt about me or the extent of the relationship you and ole girl had."

"First I never lied about how I felt about you. Keeli, keeping it 100%, when I came back in town before that nigga called me with the dumb shit, I was looking at houses for us. I was gonna ask you to come on and lets make this shit official."

"Juan get the fuck outta here." She laughed and waved me off.

"I'm dead ass serious. But when that nigga said y'all was over there sharing this lifetime together, I mean what was I supposed to do Keeli?

"I understand. You don't know how long I've wished I could go back to that night I came to your house so we could really talk Juan. Because believe it or not, you really hurt me dude."

"I believe it Ke, and for that I'm sorry."

"So you and ole girl really made a go of it huh?" Keeli asks while wiping tears away that are showing up just at the thought of him truly being with somebody else.

"I aint gonna bullshit you, we did try for a minute. When dude told me that shit, I let it drive me right back to her. Then when you showed up that night, shit fell apart between us. We tried again awhile later once I left DC, but that shit was doomed from the beginning. Both of us was too worried about you to make shit work."

"Get the fuck outta here." Keeli chuckles. "You aint gotta boost it for me babe."

"I'm keeping it funky with you. She knew I wasn't in love with her, and we both knew I was still in love with your black ass."

"Is that right?" Keeli blushes. "So where is she now?"

"In D.C I guess. But I'm telling you that's a closed chapter of my life." I told her truthfully, granted I didn't tell her why. We both just sat there I guess trying to digest all we had just given each other to chew. I couldn't stop thinking about how different shit would have been if I had just got out my chest feeling played and asked her about the nigga when he called me. I looked over at her and I could tell she was nervous and was writing her own script to what I was about to say next. I decided to go ahead and put her out her misery. "You feel like going out?" I asked her sincerely.

"Going where Juan?"

"Look just go get dressed."

"Alright."

She left the living room and went down the hall and I watched her all the way until she disappeared into one of the rooms in the back. Shorty still had the power to make me brick up instantly and I had planned to give her all this brick in a minute. While she was back there getting dressed Ciaira came out her and was all smiles. I guess her eavesdropping ass heard most of our conversation. "Y'all okay now?" Her giddy ass inquired.

"We getting there."

"Good cause I would hate for us to have to have to fuck you up Juan."

"Don't make me get Roc on you." I threw out there just to see what her response was. The smile that spread across her face told it all. My man was in there like swimwear.

"Boy bye. Aint nobody thinking about no Roc. She lied as she walked to the bar and that big ass smile never left her face. "You want a drink?"

"Yeah give me a double Hennessey." I said as I got up to go and sit at the bar with her. Once I had my drink I looked at her seriously because although Keeli and I were cool for the moment, Shorty still hadn't said shit about having my babies.

"I honestly wasn't expecting you to be in here when I came out. When I heard the door close, I figured y'all was back there giving it to each other."

"Is that right?" I laughed at her nosey ass. "Nah we about to go out for a bit, but why your girl still aint saying shit about my peoples Ciaira?" I questioned.

"Probably because she just went from ten minutes ago wanting to kill your ass Juan. Just relax, she gonna tell you. But remember you promised nigga."

"Yeah I know, but that shit should've been the first thing out her mouth."

"You will find out in time that she never does anything the way she SHOULD do it. But that's just who she is, and you gonna love her ass regardless."

I just laughed because Shorty may have been on to something. Keeli was so different from any other chick I ever encountered, and it felt like that was part of what drew me to her. I just smiled thinking about her as I downed my drink. She came back in the livingroom and had changed into some of them jeans that sat on her hips, and a white turtleneck with no sleeves and I swear I wanted to fuck her on sight. Her body was perfect in every way and I planned to get reacquainted with that work of perfection pronto. "You alright now?" Ciaira asked her.

"Yeah, I'm good." Keeli blushed at her while grabbing my hand. "You ready?"

"Yeah, lets break out. Alright Ciaira, we will check you later."

"Ok. y'all be safe." She added as she followed us to the door and locked it as we left.

We walked outside and got in my S500 coupe and I headed to the special place I wanted to take her. I had copped this spot a while ago but had never stayed there so tonight would be extra special. We talked along the way about old times, and random shit. I kept Segwaying into a conversation that would give her a clear opening to tell me she had my babies, but she never took it. That shit was mad annoying because I didn't understand why the fuck she was holding back on that.

We stopped at this little spot along the way and I got us some champagne and some flutes. Tonight was supposed to be about celebrating in my eyes and I wanted to do it right. I had my rib back and had no intentions on letting her ass slip away again.

We got out to the beach that sat behind the beach house I owned and sat out in the sand. It was dark and felt good as a motherfucka as we smoked good, drank good and talked and laughed with each other like we hadn't hurt each other and wasted time with other people. While I was enjoying the conversation and shit, I was ready to really get reacquainted. I had been watching them thick ass thighs the whole ride up this bitch and it was time now.

I reached over and grabbed her and pulled her on top of me. Without hesitation she straddled me and I pulled her lips to mine for a kiss. She had no idea how bad I wanted to taste her in every way since the minute she stepped off the plane the night before. I grabbed her shit and pulled it up, exposing her breast and they were still as I remembered them. They had grown a cup size, but she still had them big ass nipples that drove me wild. I latched on to one with my mouth and started to caress the other with my fingertips. I could feel her squeezing her legs tight because I was willing to bet that motherfucka was thumping by now. Just as I decided I was about to flip her ass over because I needed to see that fat upside down triangle

between her legs, she hopped up off me like her
ass was on fire or some shit.

"No Juan, we can't do this." She protested standing up and straightening out her shirt.

"Why? What you on your he period?" I asked trying to make sense of what the fuck she was on. Then I had to asked the obvious. "Keeli don't tell me you seeing somebody else." I stated, all while plotting on how far out into the ocean I would drag and leave her ass, and where to dispose of Ciaira body at.

"No to both of those silly ass questions. But this shit here is not right and you know it."

"What you mean?" I asked her, completely lost on what the fuck she was talking about at this point.

"So what happens after tonight Juan? I let you fuck me and then what? I'm your quarterly ho? We hook up every three months when I come to cop? She asked, sounding like she was fighting back tears.

"No! Why the fuck would you even think that? Keeli I want you. I've wanted you forever. I Love you." I pleaded with her. "We start new right now. Fuck both of our past. We build together from this moment on. Just me and you."

"That all sounds nice and what-have-you. And Juan I love you more than I think you could ever know. But I aint built for long distance relationships."

"Who said anything about a long distance relationship? You and CiCi can come here to live with me and......."

"Whoa, whoa what? So I'm supposed to give up everything and move to a country where I know nobody." She asked while looking at me like I had just sprouted eight heads. "Just leave my family and my business and all the shit that matters to me huh?"

"If you really love me like you say you do Keeli, then I don't see why that's such a problem for you." I let her know point blank.

"That shit goes two ways Juan." She walked up to me and wrapped her arms around my waist. "You can come back with me and..."

"Keeli as much as I would love to do that, I can't right now." I cut her off before we even went too far down this rabbit hole.

"Why not?"

I held her hands and looked in her eyes and it was killing me to see her look so hurt, but it was, what it was. "Keeli, baby, I can't discuss that with you right now."

"So I guess we don't love each other as much as we thought then. If neither one of us is willing to make the sacrifice to be together."

Her tears started rolling down her face and fucked me up on a level I had never felt before. She let go of my hands and turned around and started walking back up to the beach house without another word. I stood there feeling fucked up inside. I couldn't lose her again. I wasn't about to put myself through the torcher of being without her another second, so I knew what I had to do.

I took off running behind her like some shit out of a movie, but I aint care how stupid I may have looked. All I knew is I loved this woman and I wasn't about to let her get away from me again. I felt like I would literally die without her. And a nigga wanted to live ya know.

I caught up with her fast walking ass just as she had made it across my backyard and was about to walk up on the porch. I grabbed her by the arm and when she turned around with a face full of tears, not an ounce of anger, but just sadness at the thought of us not being together, I knew I was making the right choice.

"If that's what you want Keeli, you got it. Whatever it takes to make us work, I'm willing to do. I love you and refuse to let you leave my side again." I told her, meaning every word of it. She fell into my arms instantly and the smile that covered her tear stained face, I wanted to see that

smile all my remaining days by any means
necessary.

Chapter Three

That night after the beach, I fucked Keeli in a way that let her know I never wanted to lose her again. I told her 100 times while I was deep off in her shit. I was just hoping she knew how serious I was when I told her that if she ever left me again I'd kill her ass. I knew niggas said that shit daily, but I meant it from the bottom of my very soul. Especially considering the beast I was about to have to up against in order to give her what she wanted, yeah I meant that shit.

I don't remember what time we finally went to sleep, but she woke me up late in the morning to naked breakfast in bed. I couldn't do nothing but smile as she placed the tray holding the plate with pancakes and turkey bacon on it along with a cup of coffee and a glass of orange juice. She looked like something straight outta my dreams standing there with the perfect body, the perfect smile, even her flaws were perfect in my eyes. She sat the tray across my lap and then ran back downstairs to get hers and came back and got in bed with me. She blessed our food and then we started to eat. I was all smiles thinking about the future me and this woman were about to share, once I got past what I needed to do today.

"So this what I get to look forward to every morning?" I asked only half joking because I needed to know these things.

"Breakfast is the most important meal of the day baby. So you better believe yours will never come from a box in my house."

"Oh so I'm moving in with you?"

"That's what I thought. But if you want us to get a place together that belongs to BOTH of us, we can do that too. CiCi gonna trip out when he sees you."

"I was just thinking about how Ti gonna go nuts."

"I can't wait to get back home now. Do we really gotta wait out the week? I'm sooo excited baby. We can leave today."

"It aint that simple my love. I got some ends I need to tie up here first."

"That's right, go ahead and let all them hoes know their time is up. Momma's home."

"Man shut up." I laughed at her, but I knew she was serious.

"But really baby. What are we doing today? I aint never been to Panama before and I would like to see more than that wide dick before I leave… granted I plan to see that mofo again too so don't trip."

"Ha. You thought I was worried about that. You gonna be visiting with this motherfucka again as soon as I finish these pancakes. But today, I gotta handle some business. So I'mma set y'all up real good today and y'all just have fun.

"Okay baby." She said as she leaned over and kissed me. "I'm about to hit the shower. You coming with me."

"Go ahead and get started, I'll be there in a second."

I laid back watching her with genuine admiration as she collected our trays and took them back downstairs and shit. Her domesticated side was genuine and not no shit just to impress me. She could really cook, she could really keep a house clean, she could really be a good mother… not just when the crowd was watching. And I loved the fact that she was in the streets as well so she understood me. When I said I had business to attended to, there were no fake ass tears and complaints. She knew what came with the territory and respected it and I was thankful for that.

I called my personal assistant and told her I was sending the girls her way and I wanted her to make sure they had an unforgettable time. She assured me she had me covered and I didn't doubt for a moment that she did. With that, I went and met the girl of my dreams in the shower where I proceeded it fuck her until she climbed the walls trying to get away from me. I kept telling her she'd better get used to this shit because this is what she was signing up for getting with me.

Once we were finally dressed, I dropped her back off at the apartment and blessed her with my black card so they could fuck up some stores. I told her just go with the flow of what my assistant sat up for them and I would try and be back later that night… if not I would just see her first thing in the morning. Again, she assured me I was making the right choice getting with her cause she aint complain. She just kissed me and told me to be safe and she'd be waiting when I got home. That was all a nigga wanted and needed in this world. A bitch who understood, and now I had that and wasn't gonna let nothing stand in the way. Which is the reason I was about to make the trip I needed to make today.

I called the airport and told them to gas up the pacer because I needed to be in Bogota yesterday. I already knew Ian was gonna give me shit, I was just hoping shit aint explode between him and I because of what I was coming to say to him. I was gonna tell Roc to roll with me, but it felt like this was something I needed to step to my father on alone, so I did.
The 90 minutes I spent on my plane headed to see my father, I went over the things I wanted to say to him. It felt like I was rehearsing lines for a play or some shit. I was kinda glad I chose to

come alone because I needed this time to get my mind right. Ian was a tough egg to crack in a normal situation but considering all the shit I had found myself wrapped up in before I came here, I knew it was gonna be some push back. But I was on a mission. I had a whole family across the river now and I needed to be there for them.

When I got to Pop's estate, he was out playing golf. They had been able to catch him on his cell to get clearance for my plane to land. I was kinda irritated when I got in the house and he wasn't there because again he knew I was coming. I was hungry again so I had his kitchen staff whip me up some lunch while I chilled in the theater room and watched some soccer. I took my lunch and then had a nap that was well deserved right in front of the TV. When I woke up, it was fucking night time. I guess I was more tired than I realized. I went off in search of my father and found him and his newest play thing coming down the stairs heading to dinner.

"Son, good to see you awake. You are just in time for dinner. Why don't you join us? You remember Amanda don't you?"

"Yeah I do. What's up Amanda." I greeted her while she fucked me with her big ass blue eyes right there. "Pop's I was hoping I could get a few minutes with you alone tonight. It's important."

"I figured it must be if you came all the way here. I'll tell you what. Come and have dinner with Amanda and I. Once we finish our meals you and I can go talk about whatever you need to talk about son. Is that a deal?" He asked while extending his hand to me.

"Deal." I replied as I shook pops hand then followed him and Amanda into the dining area of his massive ass house. All through dinner, I didn't have much to say. This shit was just a means to an end for me, so I wasn't really interested in what pops and a bitch that he had grandkids older than were discussing. Once we were finished, Pops sent Amanda upstairs while we headed to his office on the first floor. He broke out some cigars and made us both a drink and then sat down at his massive desk. Before I could even approach the situation, he jumped right on in.

"Judging by the smile you are trying to hold in, I'm guessing the reunion went well. No?"

"What reunion pops?" I asked like a jackass, barely able to hold in my smile just thinking about her.

"Don't play with me son. You know I have eyes everywhere. Why would you think I wouldn't have any monitoring who is flying in and out to see you?"

"You and ma both always been helicopter parents." I chuckled.

"I am a helicopter. Your mother, God rest her soul, she's a fucking 747."

"She aint dead pops."

"In due time. In due time son."

"Man cut it out. The way y'all talk shit about each other every time the other one name is brought up, a man who didn't know any better would think y'all were still in love." I smirked at him cause I knew he hated when we put the two of them back in love again.

"So you came here to talk nonsense today aye?"

"Nah pops. I didn't. I came to talk to you about something serious."

"I'm all ears." Pops sipped his drink and then sat back giving me his undivided attention.

"So, the chick that showed up, that's Keeli."

"Get the fuck outta here."

"Yeah man." I laughed at how crazy everything turned out. "It turns out her ass been the one moving all that shit. BJ is her cousin and was her go between, but she the monster behind the machine." I boasted with pride.

"That's impressive son."

"Tell me about it. But outside of business Pops, I'm telling you, she's the one. I've known it since the day I met her ass."

"You think so son.'

"I'm 99% sure."

"But it's that little 1% that can be the biggest mistake of your life son."

"This is true. But that's why before I make her my wife, I need to spend some time getting to know the real her."

"Oh okay, because I'm guessing she didn't disclose to you that she was one of the biggest coke dealers on the East Coast while bouncing around on your pecker huh?"

"Nah pops, she didn't. Just like I didn't tell her that I was one of the biggest suppliers in the whole U.S during that time either."

"So you both are liars aye? You know it's hard to maintain a foundation that's built on lies."

"And I'm guessing that's why shit kept falling apart back then. But it is different now. We don't have any secrets anymore."

"So you think because now y'all have seen each other's dirty laundry y'all can make it work?"

"We got to Pops." I said sincerely thinking about the picture in my back pocket. With that, I stood up and pulled it out and handed it to my old man.

"Jesus Christ." He managed to get out while staring at the picture with pride.

"That's my legacy right there Pops. I gotta make it work for them and their sister if nobody else."

"I understand son. You know, I think about what it was like raising you and your brother and your sisters all the time. All that I have is a blessing, but none of it means more to me than the relationships I have with my children. You are my legacy and I would never keep you from yours son." He stood up behind his massive desk and outstretched his arms. "Come."

I walked over and hugged my pops and we kinda just held on to each other. I honestly thanked God every day for the relationship I had with my Pops. I knew so many niggas I met once I got to the States that never even met their fathers. I couldn't imagine my life without Ian, and it was no way I was gonna let mine have to go another day without me.

I knew from jump I was gonna have to tell him about the boys because one thing he was always about was family. Had I just been like I wanted to go back because I like the way she ride dick and scramble eggs, I'm certain he would've told me get the fuck on out his face and continue to enjoy Panama because wasn't nothing doing. But knowing he had two new grandsons on the other side of the world was all it was gonna take for him to say yes. I was still just taking in my father's embrace, when he broke the silence speaking as my Boss of sorts.

"So what happens now with her shipments." He asked as we finally separated and returned to our seats.

"As far as I know, she aint said anything about retirement. So we gonna keep that like it is. But I wanna make an adjustment on the back end of things."

"I'm listening?" Ian said as he got up to make another drink. I sat back thinking about how much his liver probably hated his ass cause Ian got it in. But only the good shit so I guess it wasn't as bad. One the flip side, I was trying to buy time because I knew I was about to sound like a whole ass OP with the shit I was about to say out my mouth. But I knew Keeli was my future and if anything ever happened to a nigga, I wanted to make sure her and our family was straight. So I took a deep breath and just spoke.
"I want her cut in on the family deal pops."

"Are you serious right now son?"
"Very much so. I told you pops shes the one."
"I hear you son. But let's not forget, Maranda was "the one" as well" He threw that out there with them funky ass air quotes and that shit hit a nigga in the chest, as I'm suspecting he knew it would. I hadn't thought about the way this bitch just up and left us after I gave her ass the world in a while. But him saying that was like snatching the bandage off hole in my heart that wasn't fully healed. I sat there for a moment lost in my own thoughts then

he snapped me back to the here and now. "Son, let me ask you this. Did you volunteer to come back or did she ask?"

"She asked Pops. As a matter of fact, she wasn't even gonna fuck with me in the biblical sense until I agreed to come home with her cause she wasn't trying to be my quarterly ho as she so kindly put it."

"Interesting. I'll tell you what son. Let me sleep on this."

"Come on pops…" I was ready to go in because I wasn't trying to hear NO at all. This shit was happening with or without his approval.

"Calm down son and just hear me out like you are asking me to do you." He came back over and gave me another drink as well because I guess he saw a nigga needed it because I was ready to spazz the fuck out. "You know how I operate and I believe in vetting people that's gonna be that close to what we have built. It was different when she was just some Chica buying coke through the pipeline, but what you are talking about now, I need to meditate and speak to the ancestors on this one."

"Really pops?" I hated when he became Colombian WOKE, that shit irritated my soul.

"And more importantly, I want you to bring her by tomorrow. Don't mention anything we have talked about please. I want to authentically meet her. Look into her eyes. Listen to her speak. Can you respect what I'm asking?"

"I can give you that pops."

"I appreciate that. Because for a second I thought I was gonna have to fuck you up in here."

"Ha. Picture that old man." I joked with my pops as we finished our drinks. When we were done we both retired to our rooms. As soon as my head hit the pillow I was about out. I called to check up on Ke and they were still out spending my money and I was 100% cool with that. I wanted her to have an amazing time for the rest of her life no matter the cost.

The next morning I was back in the air by 6am getting ready to pull this turn around. I was thankful for holding enough clout in this world to jump on my own plane and take off and land when I wanted to because all this border crossing a nigga was doing would've had all kinds of customs officials on my ass.
My driver was waiting to pick me up at the airport and we went straight to the house. I rushed in and showered and got changed while Roc finished getting himself together. I could tell he was really tryna see Ciaira because this nigga was being so extra about his attire for the day. I just laughed to myself because in the grand scheme of things, the hoops niggas would jump through for the right ones was out of this world.

Once we were dressed, my driver took us to pick up the girls, and from the moment we walked in I could tell Maria had done their asses right. They both were still fully dressed, down to the one shoe Keeli was rocking and sprawled the fuck out sleeping that good sleep. Even drunk sleep with drool on her cheeks and all this woman was flawless in my eyes.

We got them up and it took a minute for them to get themselves together but eventually they did. Once they were showered and dressed, we headed back to the airport where my flight crew was waiting for us. We boarded my plane and she was trying not to let a nigga know, but she was impressed. Not on some I'm about to run this nigga pockets type shit. It was more like she was inspired by the moves a nigga was making and wanted to step her game up. She had no idea how the moves I was planning for us together and her alone on the business side of shit would set her straight for life.

We small talked and shared laughs and shit the whole flight and the energy I got from our foursome was dope. I could see Roc and Ciaira being our go to couple, because every couple needed one. Of course our foursome would become a six piece once little brother touched down, but for the time being, I could see the four of us ruling the world together. I guess Roc was feeling the same energy because he gave me a nod that let me know our thoughts were in the same place. I just hope Ian and his ancestors felt the same wave length we were all floating on. Granted if he didn't, I had a plan B in the back of my head. I was hoping we aint have to use it though because I just couldn't see myself retiring right now and I had a feeling my other half wasn't really ready for that either.

Once we landed, Ian had a driver waiting for us and the girls rode in complete awe of what they were privy too at this point. They couldn't hide that shit as we rolled through the small town sized estate my father resided on. When we finally got to the main house, there were cars and shit parked all around the circular driveway. I just laughed because Ian aint tell me shit about he was throwing no function this day. But I knew my father well and this was his way of making sure Keeli was in a relaxed atmosphere so he could see the real her. Tensed energy lies, relaxation doesn't.

Once we got inside, the doorman escorted us onto the elevator and we headed to the roof top. Ian was pulling out all the stops today. The smoke was in the air, the pool and hot tub was damn near at capacity, the drinks were strong and the food looked and smelled amazing. I loved that my babe wasn't never shy and was ready to jump right in but I had to pump her breaks quick. She would have time to enjoy the festivities but first I needed to present her to Ian and his motherfucking ancestors.

"Boy why you aint tell us we was coming to a function." She asked as she playfully pinched me. "We aint bring our swimsuits or nothing."

"Right. Shit we tryna lounge by the water and shit too." Ciaira added.

"And what a sight that would be to see." Roc threw out there while never taking a break from eye fucking shorty in front of everybody.

"Come on, there's somebody I want you to meet." I interrupted as I grabbed Keeli by the hand and started leading her through the crowd. We got over to one of the custom hot tubs where Ian was chilling surrounded by topless chicks. My pops was out of control but he was living his life so wasn't nothing nobody could tell him.

"There's my boy!"

"What's up Papi."

"You not gonna say hello to the ladies today son."

"What's up y'all." I greeted them but was trying to keep my eyes off them the entire time because Keeli's facial expression was telling the whole story and I aint need no shit starting up between us considering we were BARELY back together.

"Hey Juan, are you joining us today?" These bitches asked me in unison, in so many words serving the pussy up on a platter. I pulled Keeli closer to me by wrapping my arm around her waist to make shit clear to these bitches because they were out of pocket.

"Papi, this is Keeli." I introduced, never acknowledging the smuts in the hot tub

"Hello." Keeli smiled, but her eyes was screaming her little ass was ready to set shit off immediately. I was both flattered and nervous because her going off was the last thing I needed to happen today. I watched Pops stare at her like he was truly in awe of her, and he probably was because she just had that kind of effect on people. He got out the hot tub and grabbed her hand and kissed it. Her ass stood there blushing at his old ass. If Slim wasn't my father I would've went the fuck off.

"You are beautiful." He told her and I could tell Ian was truly in awe of her. He had a thing for dark girls and I know that if he wasn't already hip to how I fet about Keeli he would've tried her with more than stunned admiration.

"Thank you." Her ass was still blushing.

"What the hell are you doing with him?"

"Fuck you old man." I half joked. "Seriously Papi, are you ready?"

"Si. Si. Let us go inside where we can have privacy to discuss what we need to discuss."

Pops wrapped up in a robe and then we followed him back through the crowd and back downstairs into the house to discuss shit. We got down to his office and he took a seat at his massive desk and Keeli sat across from him. I went to the bar and made us drinks while they made small talk. "Keeli, I've heard so much about you."

"Is that so." She smiled at me from where she was sitting. I gave her the panty moistening wink to let her know it was jive true, she was on my mind and I had been discussing her in her absence.

"Oh yes. My son speaks very highly of you. He tells me you are quite the businesswoman."

"I try."

"He also tells me you want him to come back to the United States with you."

"Yes. I do Sir."

"Juan, you need to come here for this."

I walked over to the desk and handed them each their drinks before sitting next to Keeli and lovingly grabbing her hand. It wasn't a conscious decision; it was more like second nature. Ian peeped it and smiled at us, I guess realizing what I felt for this woman was real shit. "What's up Papi?" I asked ready to hear what he had to say.

"I thought about this all last night and even more this morning. And I have decided to OK your plan."

"So what about the business end of things?" I asked, trying to make sure we were all on the same page.

"She buys 1200 Kilos every three months right now yes?" He turned slightly to give his attention to Keeli. "If you can move double that, I will give them to you at the family rate."

"And what exactly is the family rate?" Keeli asked.

"Five thousand dollars a key."

"Oh my God. Are you serious?"

"Very."

She sat there for a second like the calculator in her head was working overtime. Then she sat back with a concerned look on her face. "But baby, if I start to deal directly with your dad, wont that take from you?"

"Baby, I'm good. Trust me. I still got my shit going. You do what you need to do to grow your operation. Daddy good." I leaned over and kissed her softly on her lips. She never ceased to amaze me. Here she was being offered the deal of a lifetime for her business, and she was still worried about me. If I wasn't sure before about the decision I made regarding her and our future, I was positively sure at that moment.

She turned to pops not even trying to conceal her smile. "I guess we have a deal then."

"Perfect. Now let's get back upstairs and enjoy the party. We can discuss the specifics later. Come, come." Pops stood up and ushered us back upstairs to the rooftop party and we enjoyed the rest of the day.

The four of us ended up staying over that night and the next morning we flew back to Panama where Keeli and I completed our first and final deal. They stayed another three days while their shit was being put together and I would be lying if I didn't love every second of going to sleep next to this woman and her face being the first one I saw each morning. We took those three days and just continued to fall in love again, going out on dates, taking long ass walks on the beach and fucking like jack rabbits. I was trying my damndest to send her ass back on that plane with a case of morning sickness.

She still hadn't told me about the twins and I was gonna call her on it until one night she told me she had a huge surprise waiting for me at home. I was asking her for hits and clues but her big headed ass wouldn't budge. She was just like it's the type of surprise you cant tell about so I have to be patient and wait and see. I just smiled and kissed her forehead because I loved this woman so much man, and I couldn't wait to meet the perfection we created together. I never bothered to give Ciaira her picture back, I kept it in my wallet and often when I had time alone would just stare at it taking in my boys. I could see a slight resemblance to Keeli around cheeks and maybe in the shape of their eyes, but other than that, them dudes were 100% me and I couldn't wait to meet their little asses.

On the day they left, it was so hard to let her go because this girl was my everything and I really didn't want to be without her for a nano second. But I also had to do shit the right way. While I was in love and anxious to spend every day experiencing her love, I had to do shit right and handle business first. So I sent her home with a six week countdown. I still had other clientele to get straight and I also needed to make a trip out West before I went and got settled in my new life up in New York.

I spent three weeks taking care of shit with my clientele. I had them niggas flying in and out two at a time trying to make sure everybody got what they needed and was straight before I went on my hiatus. I had some serious catching up to do with my family and didn't want that shit disturbed at all. Next, I headed out West and stayed out there a week and half. My last stop before I headed up top was DC.

It felt different stepping off that plane because I hadn't been home in what felt like forever. I hadn't even told the family I was coming as I wanted to surprise them. I had two drivers waiting for us at the airport when we touched down because Roc and I needed to go two separate ways. He had folks he needed to see and so did I.

I had the driver take me directly to St. Martin of Tours Catholic School where we waited patiently. I still had some time before dismissal, and I swear it took everything in me not to bust up in there and get my baby girl. I sat there playing SODOKU on my phone and waiting for the time to pass so I could see my baby. While I was waiting, this clean ass Benz whipped into the parent parking lot and parked a few cars down from me. I was admiring the car as it got me to thinking about what kind of whip I was gonna grab for myself when out pops Sissy's bitch ass boyfriend. Why the fuck was he at my daughter school?

I sat back and watched as he went and sat on the bench near the parent pick up area. I was ready to blow because I knew Sissy aint have this nigga picking my baby up from school. Finally, the bell sounded at 2:15 and the classes started filing out. I saw my baby girl come out and she looked adorable in her school uniform. I watched Tony walk over and rap to her teacher for a second and they were all smiles. She handed him an envelope then hugged Infinity before moving on to have an exchange with another adult. Infinity grabbed Tony's hand and they started walking back through the crowd and I never took my eyes off them. My baby was getting so tall, and she looked so happy that it fucked with me. Not that I didn't want my baby to have a happy childhood. I just didn't expect... I don't know. I wasn't expecting this shit here.

I waited until they got over to the car and she was so excited talking about going to the park. I was getting ready to make my presence known then but decided to wait a minute. Besides I needed to check my own feelings about everything I was seeing before she saw me. I had the driver follow them to see what park they were going to. Once I saw where they were, I had him take me back down the street to the grocery store and I picked up some flowers and the biggest bag of Twizzlers I could find and then went back to the park.

When we pulled up, she was running and playing with a group of kids and he was sitting on the park bench reading the newspaper. I got out the truck and just stood there watching her laugh and run and yell with the other kids. A nigga had to fight back a few tears because I truly missed out on a lot during the time I was away. After watching for a few minutes, I finally went over and sat next to Tony on the bench.

"What's happening good man?" I greeted Tony as he busied himself with the sports section of his newspaper.

"Holy shit! What... what are you doing here?"

"It's good to see you too old man."
I didn't mean it like that Juan." He chuckled. "I was just shocked to see you. Sissy didn't tell me you were coming."

"Thats because she doesn't know I'm here."

"Is this safe?" He asked with concern for me etched in his face.

"Yeah. I'm good. Relax."

"Ti gonna be so happy when she realizes that you are here. She talks about you day and night literally."

"Yeah." I said feeling a mix of sadness and pride.

"Your mother is gonna go through the roof as well."

"Yeah I know."

I looked up and noticed that Infinity had stopped playing and was standing there watching us. I guess she was trying to figure out if I was really here or not. I finally stood up and she took off. She ran as fast as her legs could carry her and literally jumped in my arms. You would've thought I had just come home from the war or some shit the way my baby girl was crying. I held her so tight and had to fight back my own tears. I don't care how gangster or how deep in the streets you are, when you have a daughter, tears in her eyes be them happy or sad trumps all that gangster shit I'm telling you.

After I got her to calm down and gave her the flowers and the candy I brought for her we finally left the park and headed to my mother's house. When we came through the door she was in her favorite place, the kitchen, and whatever she was whipping up had a nigga stomach growling off the break. When I walked in the kitchen she started screaming and ran to me and hugged me just as tight as my baby girl... who was still holding on to me might I add.

By dinnertime, my mother had the whole squad at her house to welcome me back. All my sisters who were in the area, Shane, a couple nieces and nephews were all there. Since she had just been cooking a regular dinner for her house, we ended up ordering out to make sure we had enough food for everybody. We ate good, laughed and played catch up and it felt good to be home with my people and not have a feeling of dread over my shoulder. Thinking about my spirit feeling free made me think of Keeli. If it wasn't for her, I wouldn't even be here now. I couldn't wait to get home to my baby. I knew my mother was gonna have a fit when she found out why I was really here cause already she was talking about me not rushing to get a place and how I could stay there... she wanted me to stay there. I aint say shit because the whole family was around and I aint want to crush her heart, but I had to tell her eventually. The next morning, I found the perfect opportunity.

I woke up early and made my way downstairs because the smell of my mother whipping up breakfast would not let me sleep. The sun wasn't even all the way up yet, but she was up and on her shit. Once I brushed my teeth and washed my face I made it to the kitchen. Seeing my mother standing at the stove making breakfast for her family made me think of Keeli. It was so many sides to this woman and I loved them all. To know she was a monster out here in these streets getting that money AND was domesticated as fuck, that shit was a true rarity and I was so glad she was mine. I was just hoping Sissy understood and respected that shit because Keeli was it for me. I decided that night I held her in my arms again for the first time in a long time, that a nigga was done. I don't wanna be a player no more was my new theme song, and I was perfectly happy with that.

I walked over to my mother and kissed her good morning on the cheek and then made myself a cup of coffee before sitting down at the island. My mother stood there smiling at me while I sat smiling at her. Neither of us said anything for a minute or two. I guess we were both getting our talking points in order. I was ready to end the standoff and control the narrative by speaking first, but Sissy beat me to it.

"You need to call her." She said while giving me a look that let me know she wasn't asking.

"Call who ma?" I faked ignorance as to what she was hitting on.

"No, better than that, you need to go and see her. You need to go see her and explain yourself and make this right."

"Ma. That's not what I'm here for okay. Eventually, one day, I will speak to Niema. But today aint that day."

"The more I pray that you don't become him, the more you disappoint me Juan." My mother spoke sadly.

"Wow. I disappoint you now. Damn." I was truly hurt hearing her say that shit.

"Only in this situation son. That girl had to bury your son Juan. Without you. She still hasn't recovered from that."

"Why are you still talking to her and shit ma?"

"What do you mean why? Because she was almost your wife Juan! Because she gave birth to your child Juan. And you left her to deal with it all on her own."

"What was I supposed to do ma? You know how this shit goes. You were married to Pops for how long? So why you acting like you don't understand why I had to leave? The shit aint rocket science ma. The game still the same."

"And I get that Juan, trust me I do. But you didn't have to leave her out here twisting in the wind alone trying to navigate putting her first born child in the ground without you standing next to her!"

"Listen, I tried. I called her and I was…"

"You called her? You cannot be serious! What part of her child DIED do you not get?"

"Listen ma, keeping it funky, Niema knew I didn't want to have a baby with her to start with. You knew it and everybody fucking else on earth knew it. It was no secret."

"Language in my house!" She yelled at me because she had nowhere else to go in thei argument.

"You know what, maybe this was a mistake. You too caught up in somebody else feelings to get where I'm coming from, and I aint spend all them hours on a plane for this. So I'ma get Ti, and we gonna head to Tia's for the rest of my stay."

"Rest of your stay? But I thought you were back in the States for good Juan?"

"I am. But this is just a stop on the way to my final destination. I had some precious cargo to come and scoop up."

"What the hell do you mean. I know you don't mean you are taking Infinity away."

"Ma you knew this wasn't forever so cut it out."

"Where are you going? And how will you take care of her? You are always gone and traveling and out in the streets." My mother pleaded on the brink of tears.

"Ma calm down. Things are changing. Infinity will be fine. I promise."

"How! Who will take care of her?"

"She's my daughter ma and I will take care of her like I always have."

"Juan, listen to me and listen good. Infinity is at a very impressionable age where she needs stability and a constant mother figure in her life."

"And she is gonna have both of those things ma. Just chill." I got up and walked to my mother who tears had started to fall, which was pissing her off because she hated to cry… or rather be seen crying. I wrapped my arms around her in an attempt to calm her down. "Ma listen…"

"No. You listen. I love you Juan, and I love that little girl upstairs more than I can put into words. She's been through a lot and she is finally in a space where she is happy, and everything is a constant in her life. Please don't rip her from her normal because you are upset that I stayed in touch with and still care for Niema."

"Ma, I promise you, this has absolutely nothing to do with Niema. I'm taking my daughter because I'm her father and I love her. I'm trying to tell you that things are changing in my life. Seriously changing and I want my daughter to be a part of that."

"Changing how Juan?"

"I'm moving to New York Ma. So she won't even be far away. Something happened recently and I'm following my heart."

"You met somebody new Juan? That's even worse."

"She aint new ma. She's been holding onto my heart for some years now. Shit happened and we got separated but fate brought us back together and now we are making a go of it together."

"I know you are not talking about that bi…"

"Watch your mouth ma. Cause that bitch, as you were so graciously getting ready to call her, gave me something nobody else ever could."

"What? An STD?" She scoffed and rolled her eyes while breaking away from my hug.

"No smart ass." I retorted while trying not to spazz on my mother who was just being fucking difficult for no reason. "Here." I said as I went into my pajama pants pocket and pulled out the picture of the twins I still hadn't been officially told about and handed it to my mother. She stood there speechless what felt like forever just taking them in.

"Juan…."

"I love her ma. I've loved her since the day I met her. So many things happened that could've and well should've severed our ties forever. But somehow, some way fate brought us back together. And on top of that, she has my babies. Ma look at them boys." I beamed proudly.

"I know son. They are beautiful."

"I understand that you and Niema have a history. And one of these days I will speak to her. Just right now ma, I wanna focus on what's ahead of me. I want to give those boys and Ti the family they deserve. Once you get to know Keeli, ma I promise you will feel different about her."

"I won't Juan. Her energy. It's something about her that just rubs me wrong."

"Ma chill. Listen. Trust me when I tell you Keeli is good peoples. You just can't see it because you so stuck on Niema that you looked for flaws in Keeli from hello."

"That's not true Juan. It's something in her eyes and in her energy that puts me off."

"Okay ma, I aint gonna argue with you. You feel what you feel. But on the flip side, I feel what I feel and I love her ma. More than that, I am very much IN LOVE with her. I'm not asking you to write her name in the clouds on my account. I'm just asking you to respect the relationship we are trying to build. She's the mother of my sons… and please don't say nothing crazy ma cause I would hate for shit to really go left between us."

"As far as those babies are concerned, I have nothing to say but congratulations. It's clear they are your babies. But her, Juan I am telling you that bitch is bad news son."

"Ma I hear you. But I got this. Just trust me on this one please."

"You gonna do what you wanna do anyway."

"I'm glad you know that so we don't have to spend forever arguing about it."

"Okay so moving on. When do I get to meet the babies. Oh my God it's crazy how much they look like Infinity."

"I know right. But that's what I wanted to talk to y'all about as well. I got two weeks down here before me and Ti head uptop and I want y'all to come with us. Keeli and I were talking and we felt like it would be good for us all to get together.

"Um, I don't know about all of that Juan. Why don't you just bring the children here to meet your family?"

"Ma listen don't start this. It's not just the kids y'all will be meeting. She has a whole family too that going to be a part of our family in a sense. Ma I love this woman and she's going to be around so you might as well get used to it. The same way I had to get used to the fact that Tony is in your life, you have to get used to and respect that Keeli is in mine."

"Like I said it's different but whatever Juan. Have it your way. I will go for the kids. Her… Until my third eye tells me that she is not the conniving sneaky bitch that she is, I will accept that she's your woman but outside of going to meet my grandbabies initially I don't want anything to do with her."

"That's fine. Just respect that I do." I said as I kissed my mother on the cheek to calm her down because it was clear to see she was 100% upset by this conversation.

With that, I put some distance between us because it was clear she was gonna feel what she felt but at the same time I was gonna feel what I felt, and nothing was changing on either side. Again, I wasn't asking her to go and tattoo Keeli's name on her right arm, I was only asking her to give the girl a chance and respect how I felt about her. But Sissy was a stubborn one and I knew it was gonna take a miracle to get her to change her mind. I was just hoping that those twin boys I was so eager to meet was the thing to do it for her. Cause the only thing Sissy loved more than her kids were her grandkids.

My two weeks in DC flew by and I was excited to see them go. After the last conversation my mother and I had about Keeli, I opted to stay at my sister house to keep the peace. She was really in her feelings about this girl and had resulted to bringing up Niema more and more and the shit was becoming annoying. I told her several times that I wasn't ready to deal with Niema and what went down between us yet, but as soon as I was, Niema would be the first person to know. But Sissy, her ass wouldn't let up. She kept pushing the issue so by day four of my DC stay I rolled out because it was becoming too much to deal with and I was so close to Spazzing completely out on my mother at this point. But Sissy being Sissy wouldn't leave well enough alone and before I left DC to begin my new life, she was determined that I was gonna address my old one.

We had pretty much made it to the end of my DC stay and were leaving for New York in the morning. I hadn't told anyone else about the boys because Keeli ass still hadn't told me yet. Granted we talked on the phone every single day, multiple times per day but she still hadn't brought it up and there was a small piece of me that was agitated by that. But I reveled in delight knowing that tomorrow I would be holding not only my woman but my sons in my arms.

Since we were leaving in the morning, I was laying low on this day. I had been out a few times, kicked it with my niggas on the old block and the whole nine. On this day I was chilling because tomorrow was the start of a new life. Everybody was out taking care of shit before the trip, but I was lounging around my sister house enjoying the peace and quiet because I knew that shit would cease to exist as soon as I got to New York… A place I said I would never live. Yet here I was planning to live there on the wings on love. But I was lounging around the house, eating good and watching ESPN with a real live plan to do absolutely nothing, then my mother called. I started not to answer her ass, but my mother was the type that would call, then call again and then would keep on calling if you didn't answer her. I aint need that shit today. So I answered. I could hear the tears and sadness in her voice from hello."

"Hey son. Are you busy?

"No ma. Just watching TV. What's wrong?"

"I've just been thinking about everything and I really want us to sit down and talk, alone, before you make this move tomorrow."

"Ma, I'm not changing my mind about moving to New York with Keeli."

"I understand baby. And I'm not trying to change your mind any longer. I just want to talk and make sure the air is clear between you and I as well as make sure you understand why I feel all the things I feel."

"Okay ma. Go ahead, I'm listening."

"No. I want to talk to you face to face."

"Really ma? I'm chilling today."

"You have your whole life to chill Juan. Im just asking for an afternoon with my son before you run off to be a part of this woman life. Can you do that for me son?"

"Alright Ma. damn." I protested as I gave in because she was really laying the guilt on thick.

"Okay great!" Her ass perked up almost instantly and that irritated the shit out of me because it made me feel like her manipulative ass was playing me. I was ready to spaz on her ass but before I could she cut me off.

"Come over to the house, we can have lunch. I made Shepard's pie last night."

"Alright ma. Give me an hour to get myself together and then I'm headed your way."

"Thank you son. You just made me the happiest mother in the world."

Her ass was pouring it on thick and that should have been my first clue that she was on some bullshit. But like the dummy my mother made me out to be at times, I got off the phone and started getting myself together. After I showered and laid around watching a little bit more ESPN, I got dressed, hoped in my sister's Benz and headed towards my mom house. I called Keeli while I was in route to my mom's but she aint answer, I figured she was busy getting shit together for our arrival in the morning. I truly couldn't wait to wrap my arms around this woman and just hold her tight again.

My life was coming together perfectly in my eyes. I had my boy's, my daughter would be under my roof daily and now would have her own "mother" to do all the motherly shit she needed in her life. And each night when I closed my eyes, I would be closing them next to the girl of my dreams. I was on a natural high when I pulled up in front of my mother's house. It had been close to four hours since she asked me to come over and I was hungry by this point and couldn't wait to sit down at the table and dig in. I walked in the house and called out for her because I didn't see her in the living room. She yelled from the kitchen telling me where she was and that's where I headed because a nigga was ready to grub… until I walked in that bitch and there was not only my mother sitting at the center island having a glass of wine, but Niema as well.

I was caught off guard and just kinda stood there in shock for a minute because I wasn't expecting to see her. She looked different, being as though she had cut all her hair off and was rocking this super short wet look. She was still beautiful and having the baby left her with some thickness she didn't have before. For a second I felt bad about what she had experienced and the fact that she had to experience it all on her own. But then I looked at my mother who was wearing

this big ass smile and I instantly felt myself go
from feeling bad to ready to snap both their
fucking necks.

"Look who popped by to see me today Juan.
I was just as shocked as you are son."

"Ma cut the bullshit. So, you expect me to
believe that after you all but begged me to drive
out this motherfucka so we could, as you say,
talk… she just happened to pop over here at the
same motherfucking time."

"LANGUAGE JUAN!"

"Fuck that. You foul ma and you know it!"

"I did just happen to pop up today Juan, so
don't yell at Sissy like that!" Niema yelled at me.
"But when she told me you were coming over for
lunch with her, I decided to stay."

"For what?" I asked, not even feeling the
lies and bullshit she was trying to feed me as well.

"Because you have avoided me for how long
now?"

"I aint avoid you shit. I just got back in the
fucking country not even two weeks ago Niema."

"And in all that time you couldn't even
respect me enough to pick up the phone and call
me. Our son died Juan. I held his lifeless body in
my arms, alone, because we weren't important
enough for you to be there for us! It's not a day
that doesn't go by that I don't cry about my son.

About OUR SON." She expressed as tears started sliding down her face making me feel like shit.

"I never asked you for anything crazy Juan. I love you and accepted you as you are, just as fucked up as you are. When you wanted me in your life, I was there. When you needed me in your life, I was there. But when I needed you, you left me alone Juan. I had to carry that hurt alone." She started sobbing and my mother wrapped her arms around her and held her in a way, like she was trying to take away all the pain that had filled her heart at my hands.

I didn't know what to say because she was right. Niema loved me no matter how fucked up I was, and I had done her wrong. It wasn't my intention, but it just happened. I tried to feel for Niema what I felt for Keeli but it just didn't happen. Was I wrong for that?

I stood there and watched my mother hold Niema until she finally lifted her head and said she was okay. I could tell that she wasn't. I had put a lot of pain on that girl heart. Shit she would more than likely never recover from. I was hungry as fuck when I arrived, but my whole appetite was gone now. My mind kept saying just turn the fuck around and leave, but my feet felt like they had cement surrounding them holding my ass in place. It was tensed and it was awkward in the kitchen, but I found myself taking a seat at the island. I just sat there and watched my mother cover Niema with so much love and care, you would've thought this bitch was her child or something. I wondered if she would ever bless Keeli with the same kind of love she showered Niema with. I was praying she did, and sooner rather than later because again marrying this girl was deep on my heart.

My mother always used to stress to my father in the middle of their divorce that you couldn't and wouldn't have success in the next chapter of your romance if you didn't take the time and have the respect to close out the current. Although time and distance separated Niema and I, technically she was the chapter I needed to fully close out. And as crazy as it may sound, I believed in what my mom was saying. So, I took a deep breath and prepared myself to finally have that talk with Niema and put it all to rest."

"Ma, can you give us a minute?"

"Okay. I'll be upstairs if y'all need me for anything." My mother kissed Niema on her forehead then rubbed my back as she passed me on her way out of the kitchen. I sat there trying to gather my thoughts while Niema cleaned her face with a wet paper towel. She walked back over to the island and sat on the opposite side of me. I stared at her, still gathering my thoughts because I wanted to be clear as possible with her, but I also didn't want to hurt her.

For a few minutes neither of us said a word. I just kept thinking that in another life, Niema would be perfect. She was beautiful, she was smart, and she loved my ass despite all my flaws. In another life, she would be perfect. But in this life, as perfect as she was for me, my heart was somewhere else. "So what you just gonna sit there and stare at me." She asked forcing a smile to her face that didn't quite reach her eyes.

"No. I was gathering my thoughts."

"That must be a lot of thoughts. You've been quiet since Ma left the kitchen."

"I just want to make sure we clear up all this bad blood between us so we can both move on in a healthy state."

"What the fuck does that even mean Juan?"

"It means I don't want to beef with you Niema."

"I'm not beefing. I just don't understand what I ever did to you that was so wrong that I deserved to go through all I went through alone."

"Nothing Niema. I can honestly say you did nothing wrong. It was all on me. And I'm sorry for the way I've hurt you and not being there for you when the baby died."

"That was a soul crushing moment Juan."

"I can imagine. And truth be told, I was gonna leave Brazil and come be with you despite the situation I was in."

"So why didn't you?"

"When I called you, you didn't seem like you wanted me there."

"Oh hell no! You don't get to blame me for all this shit Juan! I needed you and you left me to carry it all on my own."

"I know and I apologize for that. But come on Niema, you knew I wasn't ready for a baby and…"

"Wasn't ready for a baby, or wasn't ready for a baby with me? Oh yeah, Ma told me about your boys. Congratulations."

"Niema…."

"No I get it. I wasn't good enough."

"It's not that Niema. I didn't even know about them. The situation with you is what …"

"Don't keep saying the fucking situation with me! Say what happened! Our son died! You left me stressed out and confused and our fucking son died! Say it Juan."

"Niema listen, this was probably not a good idea. You still hurting so no matter how honest I am with you about what happened, you gonna see what you want to see."

"No what it is, is that I see through your bullshit. You refuse to take any accountability for what happened and that's crazy!"

"Okay you are yelling now, so I'm done talking. You're too emotional."

"My fucking son died Juan! My son! OUR FUCKING SON DIED! Im gonna be emotional my entire fucking life while you get to run off to New York with some whore ass bitch that was a constant problem in our relationship and raise not one, but two fucking babies together. What the fuck do I get? I get to stay here and be fucking miserable and think about what my son could've been in this life, what we could've been! I get to be in constant fucking pain."

"You ever thought about seeing somebody?"

"As fucked up as I am, do you really think my focus is getting involved with another nigga to be lied to, hurt and abandoned all over again?

"I'm taking about a fucking shrink Niema."

"A head doctor? Oh okay so now I'm crazy."

"I give up! Fuck this shit!" I got up from the table throwing my hands up in frustration. "Look if you decide you wanna go to couseling and get help, reach out and let ma know and I will pay for it. Other than that, I'm done with this shit."

I started walking out the kitchen and she ran over and grabbed my shirt screaming and hitting me. It took every bit of resolve I had not to knock this bitch noodles loose, but I knew she was hurting. I tried to restrain her then ma and

Tony came running in and got her away from me. I looked at her one last time down on the floor screaming out in pain. My mother was down on the floor cradling her, she looked up at me with the saddest eyes I'd seen her have in a long time and mouthed to me "I'm sorry". I didn't say anything, I just left.

The ride back to my sister house was silent. I didn't even listen to music, just rode silently with my thoughts. It was then that it hit me that I didn't even know my son name. I didn't know where his final resting place was or anything. Although I didn't want a baby with Niema, she had my son, and he died, and I wasn't there for her in all of that. The sting of some uninvited tears started burning my eyes, but they didn't fall.

I was glad when I pulled up and my sister was home. That meant Ti was home and I wouldn't have to be alone to deal with all the shit going on in my head. I spent the rest of the evening getting ready for my new beginning and avoiding my thoughts of Niema and our son.

I was up the next morning before the sun. I can't even bullshit about how excited I was about this day. These six weeks had felt like the longest in my life and I couldn't wait to wrap my arms around my girl and look into my son's eyes for the first time. By time we got to the airport I was fueled with so much excitement I could've got out *on Route 50 and ran all the way to New York. The flight between DC and New York is one of the shortest in the world, but I promise you, the anticipation of getting to where my heart wanted to be made those 45 minutes my plane was in the air feel like 45 hours. I was surrounded by my family and I tried my damndest to be a part of the conversations and such that was filling my plane all around me, but I couldn't get my mind off of Keeli. I was legit happy and that was something I truly couldn't remember feeling like I was in a long time. I looked around at my family and couldn't wait for her and the kids to be a part of all this shit. We were a crazy bunch, but it wasn't nothing between this bloodline but love and I couldn't wait to wrap her up in it all.*

When we landed at Teterboro, I had to contain myself because I was ready to bolt from the plane and leave all their asses behind. We were greeted and loaded into the convoy of awaiting SUV's and then were on the moving. With every second closing the space between me and the girl who stole my heart with her ponytail and Reeboks so long ago. I didn't even realize how much I was smiling until my nephew was like "Damn Unk, I aint never seen you show that many teeth before. Let me find out Nanna right and shorty got a root on you." Everybody started laughing and so did I a bit. Part of it was because shorty did have me sprung out of my mind, but the other half was to keep from flipping because my mother was truly trying my patience with her bullshit and dislike for a woman she never even took the time to get to know before deciding she just didn't like her. I didn't know what it was gonna take or how I was gonna do it, but I knew I had to get my mother to see all the amazing things I saw in Keeli sooner rather than later. Not that her disliking Keeli could potentially torpedo our thing, it was just knowing that life ran a whole lot smoother when all your queens aligned, and for the most part they did. Everybody loved Keeli... except Sissy and I couldn't understand that shit for the life of me.

Before I let all that dumb shit with my mother overrun my brain, I decided to mentally check out. I sat back in my seat and anxiously took in the view leading the way to what was gonna be my new home. I was of money... hell a nigga like me WAS money, so it took a whole lot to impress me. As we moved through long Island getting closer to our final destination, I found myself impressed. Like truly impressed for the first time. Knowing all that I knew about Keeli at this space in our relationship, to know what shorty had got out in these streets and built with her own two hands from the ground up was impressive to me. It gave me admiration for her that I had never felt for a woman before, and it also gave me confidence in our future.

I knew I had a woman by my side who if the chips were ever down, she would be right there with me finding a way to pick them bitches up. I knew if something ever happened to me, shorty would make sure our kids kept living the same life they were living now. I knew that if God forbid, I ever found mysef sitting behind a wall, or laying low again, shorty could still make it do what it do without missing a beat. I was not only gaining a woman I was getting a brand-new right hand in this shit.

We got to her property and the gates were already opened for us. As the lead Suburban I was riding in rounded the corner, I saw the love of my life standing there looking good enough to eat. I couldn't wait to grip her ass and bury my dick as deep as it would go in her. These six weeks without her had a nigga going through withdrawal. Just as I felt my dick brick up with excitement thinking about getting balls deep in Keeli, I felt the blood drain from my whole body as I realized who was standing there putting one in the air with her and Ciara.

Motherfucking CoCo.

She was still as thick and as sexy as the last time I saw her. It had been quite some time, but I thought about her often. I always thought about the what if with her, but like I said before we had two different visions on life and what we wanted out of it. And her version didn't include anything long term beyond a friendship...with benefits. I was nervous as hell considering I didn't know how they knew each other, but it was clear to see her and Keeli were tight. I mean, she was all the way here in New York at an event that was for our families to get acclimated with each other. I was just praying wasn't no bullshit gonna come of this because I was here to stay and ready for this new life with her.

I decided I was just gonna play the shit cool and see what comes of it and deal with it accordingly. I was hoping I didn't have to tell her about CoCo and I because it wasn't serious and it wasn't while we was fucking around so it shouldn't even matter. However, with all my wishful thinking I was smart enough to know that her being here swapping blunt spit with Keeli on this day of all days solidified that their relationship was something solid. I was just hoping it wasn't more solid in Keeli life than ours.

I hopped out the truck with all the confidence in the world radiating on the outside, but inside, I could hear my heart thumping in my chest with the fear of what could become of this interaction. Before I could get to her, Keeli was coming at me full throttle. She dropped her blunt on the ground and all but jumped in my arms. I wrapped my arms around her and held her so tight while kissing her in a way that let her know how much I missed her ass. It felt like everybody else just faded away... until Roc blocking ass pried us apart.

"Damn nigga, you know we are standing here and shit."

"My bad." I chuckled because it was funny how her kiss pretty much made me forget these motherfuckas were here with me. "Baby, this the family." Was all the introduction I gave at the moment. I figured she would get to know each of them in her own right so a trip down the family tree wasn't necessary.

"Nice to meet you all. The party is in the backyard, you all can feel free to make yourselves at home."

"Is it females back there?" Teddy horny ass was getting started already.

"Don't start that shit today Teddy!" Moms yelled at him in her heavy accent which signaled that she was highly annoyed. Her whole fucking attitude had me wishing I had made this initial touch down on my own. I was ready to vibe, reconnect with my woman and start building a connection with my sons. I wasn't here for her bullshit.

"Ma, why don't y'all head on back to the party." I offered with my own annoyance coming through in my voice.

"We don't know where we are going. This aint our house." Ma snapped back at me and as much as I love her ass, I was ready to take the kind gloves off.

"Is everything ok?" Ciaira asked with a sweet smile trying to diffuse a situation that was clearly about to get out of hand.

"Everything is fine." Keeli tossed in matching her smile while rubbing my back lovingly. "Can you show them to the party please."

"Not a problem." CoCo chimes in.

"Follow us please." Ciaira said extra bubbly.

The family split up and the crew that was staying with us all stayed behind to go get situated with their luggage while everyone else including my mother followed Ciaira and CoCo into the house and out to the party. We all followed Keeli around her massive home as she showed folks where they would be staying. I loved that she was genuinely happy to not only have me here but my family as well. Her and Shane were all over each other with pure joy at being reunited. I was also glad she was so focused on my family because that kept her from seeing the looks CoCo big fine ass was shooting me before she left to show my family around. I was praying that everybody else had missed that shit as well. I knew I was gonna have to have a conversation with her because it was no way Keeli could find out about what she and I used to share.

Once we finished dropping everybody off at their rooms, we finally made it to her master suite which sat at the end of the hall behind a huge set of double doors. I kicked off my shoes and went and got right on top of her custom Cali King. She looked amazing standing there with her side ponytail, stealing my heart all over again. I noticed for the first time that she looked nervous, and I kind of already knew why. She was probably trying to figure out how to tell me about the boys. I decided to Segway her on in, trying to make what had to be complicated for her just a tad bit easier.

"Why you all the way over there? We aint seen each other in 6 weeks. I know that thang throbbing for Papi to get in it." I asked as I pulled her close to me on the edge of the bed. I kissed her so deep I could feel the goosebumps forming on her body. She was melting in hands and it felt so good just to be with her again. I wanted her so bad, but I also wanted to meet my sons. I started rubbing up her thighs thinking hell, I've waited all this time to meet them, another 30 minutes aint gonna hurt. I needed her right now. I legit hadn't been with nobody else since the night her ass stepped off that plane and stepped back in my life. So I needed her bad right now. Six weeks was a long ass time for a nigga. Just as I got to the promise land, she pumped my breaks.

"As bad as I want you balls deep inside of me right now, it gotta wait. I got some people I want you to meet."

"They can wait baby. I NEED to feel you right now Ke."

"Not these people baby." She offered in a serious tone as she slid out the bed and started fixing her clothes. "I'm gonna run out and get them. Grab TiTi and wait for us right here please.

"Alright." Was all I was able to get out cause I promise my dick was so hard I could barely speak. I was torn between the excitement of meeting my sons and the pain of having my shit left on pause like that.

"Don't worry Papi. I promise you we gonna make this a night to remember." She winked at me and then turned and took all that jiggle on out the door leaving me alone with a swollen dick.

I laid there for a few minutes thinking about anything that could help redirect the blood that wasn't flowing through my body.

Finally, I was able to focus and got up and moved my luggage out the doorway where I left it at. I figured I would unpack things later. I left the master suite and went back down the hall to the room TiTi was in. When I walked in she was unpacking her clothes and placing them in drawers. Keeli had told her this room was only temporary. Her actual room had been stripped bare because she wanted her to decorate how she wanted it. I loved that it was important to Keeli to make sure my baby not only had her own space but her own representation in the house.

I stood and watched my baby girl for a minute or two undetected. I worried about TiTi a lot. Although she had a lot of women in her life, she didn't have her mother and that was all I wanted for her was to have that bond with a mother. I got that my mother was feeling whatever she felt about Keeli, but in my heart of hearts I felt like she was what both TiTi and I needed."

"Hey daddy. Everything okay?"

"Yeah Babygirl. Everything is fine. You getting settled in okay?"

"Yeah. I'm hungry though and whatever they grilling smells so good."

"Well save unpacking for later. Keeli wants to introduce us to some people and then we gonna go grub and enjoy the party. You have forever to unpack."

"Okay." TiTi offered with a smile as she bopped over and grabbed my hand and we headed back down the hall to the Master Suite. We went inside and I sat down on the sofa while TiTi walked around taking in what was now her "Parents room".

"So how are you feeling about this move Babygirl. And be honest with me."

"I'm always honest with you daddy." TiTi shot back sweetly and I just wished I could bottle her up and keep her as the amazing little girl she was today. "I'm excited. It's gonna be fun living with you all the time. Having a mom and having a brother."

"Wait, so you already know?" I quizzed, partially ready to go off on my mother for telling her about the boys.

"Of course I know Keeli is not my real mom daddy." She rolled her eyes at me. "I'm not a baby. And I know CiCi is not my real brother. BUT, when you marry her she will be my stepmom. You are gonna marry her right?" She asked as she came and sat down on the sofa next to me.

"You think I should Babygirl?"

"Yes. I think you should. "

"In due time Babygirl." I offered her with a kiss on her forehead. "In due time."

Just then Keeli walked back into the suite followed by CiCi and they each were carrying a twin. In the time I had known Keeli, I had never seen her look as vulnerable and nervous as she did

in this moment. While TiTi was wrapping CiCi up
in I miss you hugs, Keeli stood there looking at me
like she was trying to will a smooth encounter with
this situation. She had no idea that I was about to
fucking burst with excitement finally having laid
eyes on my seeds. They were perfect in every
way.

"Baby, these are the two people I couldn't
wait for you to meet. These are the twins. Ishmel
Jalen and Mecca Jamel."

I got up from the sofa and walked over to
her wearing a smile I couldn't wipe off my face if I
wanted to... not that I wanted to. I stood there and
towered over her little ass and tiled her chin
forcing her to look up at me. Her eyes were
welling up with tears and I couldn't take seeing her
stress over what's next a second longer. I leaned
in and kissed her. It wasn't sexual. It was more like
a connection kiss. It was a kiss to say thank you for
completing me in every way. Thank you for
completing me in ways that I didn't even know I
longed for. After I kissed her, leaving her little ass
breathless, I finally spoke wearing a huge kool aid
smile. "So why didn't you tell me?"

"I was still upset. Plus, I didn't know how to
tell you. I didn't know how you was gonna react."

"How old are they?"

"15 months. They were born March 9th,
1996."

Hearing that date again hit me hard. I mean yeah, I knew when they were born because Ciaira had told me. And I knew that was also the day my son with Niema died. But it was something about hearing out of her mouth that they were born on March 9th that fucked with my heart. I didn't even realize my emotions were showing until I noticed the smile was gone from Keeli's face and replaced with a look of sadness.

"Look babe, I know this was a big surprise. If you want a blood test I completely understand and will arrange it and pay for it immediately." She offered on the brink of tears.

"Man shut up." I laughed in an attempt to ease her fears and uncertainty.

I pulled her and my son she was holding into a loving embrace to let her know I was here, and everything was alright. Then I pulled CiCi and TiTi along with the other twin into our family hug. I was complete. We were complete. And felt good.

Our family reunion was going so well, we damn near blew off the party that was happening out back. It wasn't until Ciaira and Roc showed up together to drag us back down to the party that we returned. I was feeling good when I walked out onto the deck carrying both my sons and their mother standing at my side. I couldn't wait to walk them around and introduce them to everyone. The only person I was worried about was my mother. Although we had talked about the fact that Keeli had my sons, Sissy could be a real piece of work at times, and she had been going hard so to make her position on me and Keeli known that I wasn't too sure that her newest grandsons wouldn't become collateral damage in the midst of all this. I loved my mother but I was praying she wasn't on no fuck shit like that. Because while I loved and respected her, it was my duty to not only love and respect Keeli and my boys, bit to protect them as well. So I wasn't for her reckless mouth and bullshit.

Keeli and I made our rounds introducing my sons to everyone and it was all love. Even with my mom. She was all over the boys the minute she got her hands on them. I was so wrapped up in loving on Keeli, meeting her family, playing with my sons and eating like a champ that I had completely managed to forget about the elephant in the room..

Motherfucking CoCo!

I wasn't sure where she had been hiding at since I first saw her when we got there, but I promise the entire time we were out partying I didn't see her again. It wasn't until the party was winding down that she and I crossed paths again. Keei and I had taken the boys upstairs to get them cleaned up and put them to bed. Ishmel was out as soon as his little ass got out the tub, but Mecca drove a hard bargain. Keeli said this was normal with him. He believed in fighting until the very end. I found myself laying on the floor chest to chest with him while patting his back to try and get him to go to sleep. Keeli sat in the rocking chair wearing this huge smile on her face while watching me like a hawk. I didn't know what she was thinking, but other than how hard I was gonna fuck her as soon as this damn boy went to sleep, my only other thought was how happy I felt for the first time in a real long time.

"What you staring at?" I joked with her.

"You. Fatherhood looks soooo sexy on you."

"Is that right?"

"It is. A person would never think this was your first time meeting the boys. They just took to you immediately. And your family baby. These dudes usually don't like anybody babe."

"That's cause they know their family."

"I really never thought this day would come baby. You have no idea how many nights I held them wishing you were a part of this."

"Well I'm here now baby. And I aint going nowhere."

"You promise?" Keeli asks as she laid down on the floor next to me and snuggled in my arms.

"I said it didn't I?" Keeli knew my word was my bond and I didn't say shit I didn't mean. I kissed her forehead and managed to grab a handful of her ass. "You know I'ma fuck the shit out of you tonight right?" I asked, barely able to contain myself.

"You know I'ma let you right." Her goofy ass laughed.

"You think I'm playing. But I suggest you make tomorrows bottles and shit tonight for them and show somebody where everything at because I doubt you leaving the bed the next day or two. You got six weeks to make up for. You think that motherfucka fat now. Just wait til I get finished beating up on her."

"Oh my god you so nasty. That shit making me so wet."

"Let me feel it"

"Boy no. Mecca ass is laying on you."

"He damn near sleep babe. Just don't be loud if you start to cum." I instructed as I slid my hand into her jumper, moving her panties to the side and caressing her swollen clit.

I could tell by the way her breath got caught in her throat she was gonna cum quick. I readjusted Mecca who was 33 seconds away from sleep, so if he happened to pop back up he wouldn't catch his mother having an out of body experience. The deeper I rubbed, the wider she spread her legs until I had full access to her opening. I slid two fingers deep into her and held them still causing her to bite down on her lips in full ecstasy. I didn't even have to stroke her at this point. I rubbed her clit while she rotated her hips, grinding her pussy on my fingers.

I rolled Mecca ass off me and onto the floor because I couldn't take it any longer. She was about to cum and I wanted to fully be a part of that. I got up on my knees and stared into her eyes while she worked the shit out of my fingers until she couldn't take it anymore. Right as she reached her peek I brought pressure down on her kissing her in an attempt to cover her mouth because I knew this was intense, while I fucked her hard with my fingers. The only sounds in the room was wet pussy and heavy breathing and that shit damn near drove me mad. I was damn near ready to cum in my own pants. My dick was so hard, it hurt at this point. I finally pulled my soaked fingers out of her pussy and sucked off all the juice she had given me.

"So that's how you feel huh?" She asked, barely able to catch her breath.

"Put him in the bed and meet me in the room now. I NEED that little fat motherfucka right now."

"Your wish is my command." She tossed at me as she got up on her knees and kissed me. As we were in the middle of sharing the taste of her pussy on my lips, the problem I kept forgetting I had walked in the room.

"This why can't nobody find your ass." CoCo barked as she came in carrying the same loud ass tone I had always known her to carry.

"Bitch I know you better hush before you wake them." Keeli snapped at her.

"Anyway. We all getting ready to roll out so Dana said you can play with dick later, you need to come and say bye to your family."

"Aint nobody even..." Keeli protested.

"Girl, tell me that shit with your pussy aint hanging out our damn clothes." CoCo laughs

"Whatever bitch." Keeli laughs as she stands up and adjust her clothes then looks at me. "Babe will you please put him in the bed so I can go say bye to these people."

"I got you baby. Do your thing."

"I'ma say bye to my babies then I'll be down there." CoCo offered as Keeli exited the room leaving us alone for the first time in years. We both stood there in silence for a minute, I guess giving Keeli enough time to get out of earshot before we addressed this situation. I picked

Mecca up off the floor, thankful for the plush carpeting that comforted him while Keeli and I did us. I laid him down in his crib then turned to face CoCo who was standing there watching me with so much intensity.

"Who would've ever thought?" She snickered while biting her bottom lip.

"Tell me about it."

"When I saw you step out that truck today, I almost passed out."

"Shiit, how you think I felt. The last person I expected to cross paths with today was your ass."

"Yeah, I haven't seen you since you rolled out in the middle of the night, leaving me with that little package you left me with."

"Yeah about that. I swear I didn't know until after the fact and..."

"So we both clear that you gave that shit to me right and not the other way around." She snapped at me, and it was part of me that wanted to smack the shit out of her, but I knew it wouldn't go over well.

"Yeah and again I apologize. That was not intentional and like I said I didn't know. If I did, I wouldn't have even come over then."

"Um huh." She rolled her eyes and circled me like a shark. "So how long you been fucking my little cousin."

"Little cousin?"I hated the way she tried to use little in an attempt to belittle Keeli and place her beneath her.

"Yes. Keeli is my little cousin. Her mother and my mother are sisters."

"Wow, small world."

"Extremely." She rolled her eyes and walked over to Ishmel's crib and rubbed his face gently. "It's crazy now looking at them and looking at you, it's clear to see who their dad is."

"Oh what you thought it was somebody else?" I pried to see if Keeli was truly keeping it a buck with me.

"Don't do that okay."

"Do what?"

"Let's not play this game Juan okay? You and Keeli have what y'all have and we had what we had. I just wanted to make sure we cool and on the same page about not sharing this with her."

"No arguments here."

"I guess this is why as bad as I wanted you, I couldn't allow myself to let go and be yours."

"Yeah. Life is funny like that."

"So let me ask you this..." I knew she was coming with the bullshit the way she slid up in my space making us close enough that I could feel her big ass nipples graze my arm as she brushed up against me. "Are we really done? Or are you down to rekindle what we had? I mean, we kept it just between us all that time. So just let me know what we are doing. I know you miss all this." She grabbed my hand and stuck it between her thick warm as thighs and all I could think about was the way this bitch used to do full splits on the dick.

It took everything in me, but I managed to find the will to pull my hand from between her thick,soft ass thighs. "Co, what we had back then was bomb. You've done some shit I'll probably never experience again in life with your freaky ass. But not only do I love Keeli, I'm in love with her ass."

"You sure?" She asked looking at me intensely.

"I'm positive." I said honestly.

"I was hoping you said that Juan." She moved in and hugged me. "You got a good one, and although she's my cousin. I love her like a sister. So please treat her right because she deserves it and that girl loves you more than I think you'll ever be able to understand."

"I got you CoCo. I promise I got you."

Just then Keeli walked back in the room and for a second, I felt the blood drain from my body feeling like I was caught and she was about to go OFF as most women would walking in on their man hugging their fat booty, freak ass cousin. I was scared shitless thinking I had just blown it. Then CoCo turned to her and smiled all while still hugging me. "Hey Boo. I was just on my way downstairs. You know I had to come and kiss my boys before I left."

"You know Ish gonna get up looking for you in the morning."

"I know, but duty calls." CoCo finally let go of me leaving me standing there looking like a fucking idiot. "Well it was good meeting you Juan. I'm glad to have you as a part of our family. And remember what I said... treat her right or I'ma be on your ass I promise."

"CoCo get out!" Keeli laughs while finally grabbing her cousin and pushing her towards the door.

"Love you Boo."

"Love you more. See you in a few weeks."

"Bye CoCo." I tossed out as she walked out the door as a way to be a part of the conversation on some level.

I just didn't want Keeli to get suspicious, because although my shit with CoCo was before her, she didn't strike me as the kind to stick around if she knew about the shit. So for that reason, I had to omitt the bit of info and keep the shit omitted until the end of time.

Keeli walked up and wrapped her arms around me and I kissed her on her forehead. She looked up at me and smiled in a way that was so innocent and so full of love. I had been wanted by many women in my lifetime, but this here was something different. This was destiny and a nigga was all in for the shit.

After Keeli and I saw her family off, as well as my family that wasn't staying we finally made it upstairs to the bedroom. We took a bubble bath together and we tried to make it to the bed but the wanting was too much and I ended up folding her ass up right on the floor in front of the entrance to the private bathroom and fucking her like my life depended on it. When it was over, I lead her to the bed and climbed in behind her. She laid her head on my chest and we both were out of it.

I went to sleep that night floating on a cloud, or at least that's how it felt. Many things had tried to stand in our way, but somehow, we had overcome them all and now we were here. Together.

Sure, hearts had be broken along the way but that was life. Keeli and I being together was fate, and one thing for sure was you can't stop fate.

Unfortunately, just as you can't stop fate, you cannot stop the consequences attached to your fate. And as I laid there that night, wrapped in the bliss of finally and truly being with Keeli, I had no idea just how dire the consequences of my fate would be in the end...

The

Consequences

of

Loving

The

Queen

of

DC

Available Summer 2020

Please Enjoy This Preview of....

Twas the day before Thanksgiving...

I had been looking forward to this day for the past two months. From September to today, it felt like I had literally been working around the clock. 12 hours a day, 6 days a week had taken a whole toll on my mental and it felt like my physical as well, but it was for a good cause. Today was the start of my official holiday season and I had plans. Between making my babies eyes light up on Christmas morning and our first family vacation in years a bitch needed MOOLAH. So, I held it down and did what I had to do. Today was Wednesday and I didn't go back to work until next Wednesday, so I woke up smiling to the sound of no alarm. It had been forever since I had done that.

I got up then got my daughter Saneeah and my son Ashland up because we needed to hit the store to get the last minutes things for the festivities. At 13 and 10, they were at ages where I actually loved having them accompany me to the store. They were passed the "mommy can you buy me" with every corner we turn stage. Now they were helpful more than anything. So I was happy to have them tag along and help me in the grocery store and getting the rest of our decorations for the tree and such.

Our holiday routine was important to me. My kids were growing up fast and it wouldn't be long before I looked up and they were grown. So I tried to spend every moment I could bonding with them over whatever I could. Aside from them growing like weeds, my son had sickle cell anemia and the past two years had been extremely hard for him. He had been fighting this battle his whole young life, but the past two years his admissions to the hospital had been frequent. Thankfully, he was doing good right now and that was all the more reason I wanted this holiday season to be extra special for my babies. They were everything to me, and at times they felt like they were all I had, despite me having a whole ass husband.

Some days, I would literally sit and ponder trying to figure out exactly why the fuck did I get married. I loved Saneeah with all that I was but the fact that if I hadn't got pregnant with her, I'm 99.9999999999% positive I would've never married their father often looms in the back of my mind.

I came to DC for college. Going to Howard had been my forever dream. I had my whole life planned out before I got finished with middle school, and truth be told this wasn't it. I had the potential to do ANYTHING. I graduated high school with honors and had my pick of 12 phenomenal schools. Howard was my first choice and I took off running from Tallahassee to DC on the first thing smoking. My parents wanted me to go to school close to home, but since they weren't paying for it, I didn't give them that control over my life. They had been controlling things from day one. This was me asserting the fact that I was grown by taking off for DC all smiles.

I met Ash before my damn suitcase even stopped rocking. He was working at the McDonald's on Georgia Avenue which was pretty much on campus. I was pressed for a job because my life had been school, school, school and it was clear I was gonna need a little money to handle living in DC. True enough I had free room and board in my academic scholarship, BUT DC was a town of life and a bitch was ready to live. I knew I was gonna need a lil money to shop at *Up Against the Wall* and all the stores that lined Georgia Avenue so I applied for McDonalds and got the job.

By the end of my first part time week, me and Ash were in a relationship. By time I went home for Christmas break, I was hiding the fact that I was pregnant from my parents. Man, you couldn't tell my dumb ass that we were not gonna make it. The magic my dumb sheltered ass was making in my head with them two little McDonald's paychecks was out of this world! By time Spring Break rolled around, I was ready to be grown and tell my folks so me and Ash took the Greyhound from DC to Tallahassee, so we could announce our pregnancy and engagement to my parents. I will NEVER forget the hurt in my father's eyes as he smelled the bullshit when we walked through the door. Next thing I knew he was kicking Ash's ass all over our yard. Me thinking I was grown and defending my soon to be husband turned my back on my whole family. They didn't know our love…. Yeah that's the bullshit I was seriously telling myself. Our trip to the sunshine state was immediately over and we went back to DC on some real live Bonnie and Clyde shit screaming fuck the world.

My mother showed up in DC two weeks later only to find out I had flunked out of school. My dumb ass let him convince me that I needed to push college to the side and focus on getting that French Fry check so we could be straight by time the baby came. She came to my job and that was the first time we talked since her husband attacked mine…. Oh yeah, I was Mrs. McCheese the day after we got back to DC. We went out to Virginia, just me and him and said our I Do's. I was truly in a fog, following his dumb ass lead. But my mother begged me to just come home. Let her and my father help me with the baby, and get me back in school locally in the coming fall. My mother, a woman of grace and pride got down on her knees in McDonald's and cried her heart out begging me to come home. I looked at my mother and my young ass confused love for what I thought was disappointment and looked over at Ash and confused pure fuck-boy-ism for what I thought was love, and with that I walked away from my mother to join hands with my husband and walk to the bus stop because his shift was over.

A week later we welcomed Saneeah came screaming into the world.

I knew on some level I had made the wrong choice in life, but my pride wouldn't let me suck that shit up and take my baby and go on home to my family and get back on track. I convinced myself that Saneeah needed her dad, and as his wife I was forced to deal with the good times and the bad. I mean, I get that and all, but the bad times started coming from before the ink dried all the way on our marriage license. With him bouncing around from job to job, battling it out with his family, a side bitch or two…Oh yeah, he had the audacity to go fucking around more than once. Like nigga we are living in your grandma living room at this point and you got time to go fuck off. But now here we were, 13 years and two kids later.

I eventually got my shit semi together after dead end job after dead end job and went on TANF when I got pregnant with AJ. While I was on it, I went to school for medical assistance. Graduated, had him, dealt with his health issues for two years. Finally got a job at a clinic as a pediatric nurse assistant. Ash got hired as a supervisor for a janitorial company cleaning the court complex out in Fairfax and we were doing okay. It was like finally we were getting shit in order.

After both of us holding shit down for two years we were in a semi good space. We jumped out there and decided to buy a house together. Call me crazy but I was excited. We were grown and had never lived on our own. When I left college, I moved in with him and his stupid ass mother. And I was ready to go within a week. We lived with her until Saneeah was about 3 months old then me and her had a real live fist fight because she burnt my baby with a cigarette. Like why the fuck are you even smoking in her presences? But then we stayed with his aunt for a year, but she was so scared somebody wanted her drunk ass boyfriend that we ended up leaving there and staying with his Grandma until we brought our home out in Capitol Heights.

I loved it because it was ours first and foremost. My kids could move about freely and so could we. Ash never had issues wherever we went because it was his family and they loved him…. But they aint fuck with me too tough. They actually felt like I trapped him and got pregnantt on purpose JUST so he could marry me. They were quite the delusional bunch. I missed my family like crazy, but pride was a motherfucka and I refused to let them know they had been right about me marrying him being the biggest mistake of my life....

Available Fall 2020